Sheri Marsh stared in blank amazement at her official nightmare come a-calling—the infamous Matchmaking Posse of Mule Hollow.

"Okay," redheaded Esther Mae Wilcox was saying. "We made a list of all the single cowboys." She paused, as if waiting on an imaginary drumroll. "There's still some great pickin's out there. You needn't worry you're getting the runt of the litter."

That did it! Sheri bolted up from the table so fast it shook. "You have all had your fun," she said. "But for the last time, lay off. I am more than capable of finding my own cowboy. If and when I'm interested in finding him—"

"Well, we never said you couldn't find *a* cowboy," Esther Mae interrupted. "You just can't seem to find the *right* cowboy. You know, *the one…*"

Books by Debra Clopton

Love Inspired

DEBRA CLOPTON

was a 2004 Golden Heart Award finalist in the inspirational category. She makes her home in Texas with her family.

Meeting Her Match
Debra Clopton

Steeple
Hill®

Published by Steeple Hill Books™

STEEPLE HILL BOOKS

Steeple
Hill®

ISBN-13: 978-0-373-87438-5
ISBN-10: 0-373-87438-3

MEETING HER MATCH

Says the Lord, "You will seek me and find me
when you seek me with all your heart."
—*Jeremiah* 29:13

This book is dedicated with much affection and
admiration to Mitzi Poole Bridges.
Without your encouragement
I might have given up...thank you.

Chapter One

Says the Lord, "You will seek me and find me
when you seek me with all your heart."
                                        —*Jeremiah 29:13*

Sheri Marsh stared in wide-eyed amazement at the
three women around the table with her at Sam's Diner.
They were her official nightmare come a-calling.

Oh yes, it was true. These deceptively innocent-
looking little old ladies were the infamous "Matchmaking Posse" of Mule Hollow. And they'd just informed
Sheri that they had a plan to wipe her woes away.
Whether she wanted them to or not!

"Okay," Esther Mae Wilcox was saying, her hands
held out in front of her as if she were about to deliver
the biggest punch line of all time. "So, are you ready?
Here's the plan." She paused, as if waiting for an imaginary drumroll. "Me and Norma Sue made up a list last
night. And Sheri, you are just going to *love* it!"

Well, Sheri thought, looking at the bright side, at least the truth was on the table now—no more hints, no more hemming and hawing. The posse had come clean. They'd admitted what she'd already deduced was going on behind her back.

They were setting her up!

Tamping down her escalating temper, Sheri leveled her gaze at each of the women at the table.

First she zeroed in on Esther Mae. The woman was like Lucille Ball and her sidekick, Ethel, rolled into one.

Then Sheri shot her gaze to Esther Mae's partner in mayhem, Norma Sue Jenkins. She had a very full figure and the willpower of a steamroller. Sheri could just see herself looking like a flattened Gumby after Norma Sue got through plowing over her with her matchmaking notion.

Last but not least, Sheri settled her gaze on Adela Ledbetter, a wisp of a woman who balanced the other two out with her serenity and godly wisdom. Okay, she usually balanced them out. At the moment, to Sheri's dismay, she wasn't balancing anything with that soft smile and twinkling eyes! Nope, Sheri could tell that obviously Adela had more important *personal* things on her mind, like the cute-as-a-wrinkled-raisin Sam, owner of the only diner in the rustic town of Mule Hollow, Texas.

Yep, Adela was just sitting there letting Sam place a steaming cup of coffee in front of her, *in the special china cup that Sam used only for Adela.* It was no secret that there was romance in the air between the spry proprietor and the truly special lady. In fact, nobody seemed to understand what was keeping them from taking the trip to the wedding altar. Plus, unlike the way they'd latched on to Sheri, her cohorts didn't seem in any hurry to tie Adela and Sam up in a neat little match-made-in-Mule-Hollow-heaven package. And as far as Sheri was concerned Adela and Sam needed some help. At the pace they were going they'd be batting eyes at each other forever. They'd never experience wedding bliss unless someone stepped up and lit a fire beneath them.

Sheri bit her lip. Was it too much to ask that the focus be taken off her single status and applied to Adela?

Lastly, Sheri glared at her best friend, Lacy, who was sitting on a stool at the counter and had spun to face them. She was just as intent as the senior posse on trying to find Sheri a husband. Her mischievous grin and laughing eyes proved it as she met Sheri's glare.

"What we did," Norma Sue continued, drawing the words out as if she were about to make a major proclamation, "was make a list of all the single cowboys. Then we listed all their truly wonderful attributes. Let me tell you, Sheri, there's still some great pickin's out there. You need not be worried that you'll get the runt of the litter."

"That's right," Esther Mae broke in. "After all, love is a very idiosyncratic view—"

"A *what?*" Norma Sue exclaimed.

The previously full-figured Esther Mae threw her recently achieved size-twelve shoulders back and looked down her nose at Norma Sue. "I-di-o-syn-cratic," she said slowly, as if pronouncing it to a child. "It means subjective." She smiled proudly, ignoring

Norma Sue's frown. "I'm learning new words out of the Reader's Digest. It's supposed to keep my mind alert, so y'all get ready. I'm gonna be bustin' them out on occasion. You know, when the opportunity arises."

Sheri joined everyone in staring openmouthed at Esther Mae. It was a known fact that Esther Mae couldn't get the words she already knew into the right context. Where she'd go with bigger, better words was anybody's guess.

"I think that's a grand idea," Lacy said at last, breaking the silence. "You learn them first then teach us."

"Are you crazy?" Norma Sue asked incredulously, finally finding her voice. "Esther Mae—"

Esther Mae harrumphed. "Now you just hush, Norma Sue Jenkins. Just because I get a word tangled up here and there is no call to get in a tizzy."

Sheri wanted to laugh, but she didn't dare call attention to herself. At least for the moment they weren't focusing on her and the list of local eligible bachelors.

"That's right, ladies," Adela chimed in, reeling her friends back in. "Nobody's crazy. Now back to the topic at hand…. Sheri, I'm sure that you know love is a lasting connection that God orchestrates between a man and a woman. We're simply nudging people in the right direction. No one can actually understand the mystery that binds couples together except the two people themselves."

Well so much for being out of the hot seat, Sheri thought drily.

"True, that brings us back to our list." Norma Sue slapped Sheri on the back and smiled her mile-wide smile. "The best thing for a broken heart is to get back in the saddle, and so we think we've got the field narrowed down for you. I have to tell you that it hasn't been an easy job. You know as well as we do that there's not just any man out there who can keep up with you, Sheri Marsh."

Lacy grinned. "I think most of the guys are scared of you."

Esther Mae halted her forkful of apple pie midair. "That's probably right. I asked Simon Putts about takin' you out on a date—you all should have seen his face. He went pastier than Norma Sue's dumplings."

That did it! Sheri bolted up from the table so fast it shook. She couldn't take Esther Mae asking somebody on a date for her. And Simon Putts of all people? Why, the name fit him like a glove. "Okay, listen up," she said. "You all have had your fun, but for the last time lay off me. I am more than capable of finding my own cowboy. If and when I'm interested in finding him—"

"Well, we never said you couldn't find a cowboy," Esther Mae interrupted. "You just can't seem to find the *right* cowboy. You know, *the one*. We know your heart was broken—"

It was Sheri's turn to interrupt, frustrated beyond words. "Okay, okay. Yes, my heart is hurting because of J.P. I hope you're all satisfied that I'm admitting it." She was steadily backing toward the door, feeling as if a noose was tightening around her neck. She needed her freedom. "And since my heart was broken, that should make you realize I'm not, and I repeat once more, I am *not* looking for *the one*. I'm not looking for anything. Goodness, y'all, I'm kinda confused right now." There, she'd admitted more than she wanted, and they were still looking at her as though she was the next star of their runaway hit, *How to Marry Off a Girl in Ten Days Whether She Wants to Or Not!*

Just in the nick of time she bumped into the door.

"What's your hurry, Sheri? You don't have a pedicure for another hour," Lucy said.

Sheri glared at her soon-to-be former best friend Lacy, pushed the swinging door open and spun through it. Lacy's chuckles followed her out to the sidewalk.

They were out of control! Really. This was just not right. Happy single people ought to have the right to walk the streets of Mule Hollow just like everyone else. That's right, without the worry that they were going to be unduly set upon by the matchmaking posse. Somebody should do something about it. People could get hurt...*like her!*

Why, it just wasn't right for them to think that everyone in Mule Hollow was their own special puppet, to be led here and there as they saw fit. Sheri marched down the sidewalk indignantly. How would they like it if the tables were turned on them? They wouldn't like it one bit if a person manipulated them! Oh, no, they wouldn't. It would serve them all right if someone pretended to fall in love because of their scheming. Just when the posse began to pat each other on the back they would find out the joke was on them.

That's it!

Sheri stopped dead in her tracks. Her anger dissipated as she thought about what just flashed through her thoughts.

It was a brilliant plan.

A way-past-time-for-it kind of plan.

But it seemed deceitful. The thought dimmed her initial pleasure. Then again, she told herself, this was a lesson the ladies needed to learn. And it seemed that they would only learn it through something as drastic as her budding plan…since they certainly weren't hearing what she had to say.

It was true. Sheri stood in the center of Mule Hollow's Main Street, gazing down the colorfully painted buildings lining both sides of the street. She had to admit…there hadn't been a shake-up like this could be since Lacy came to town and painted the two-story beauty salon flamingo-pink, then followed it by talking everyone into painting the rest of town all colors of the rainbow.

It had been the lonesome town's single cowboys who'd been shook up on that day. But this, this plan would shake up the matchmaking posse so they would leave her alone and quit plotting the demise of her single status.

Getting back in the saddle was how Norma Sue had put it. Well, for a girl who'd loved being in the saddle until J.P. threw her off, she was struggling on new terrain here and they weren't helping.

She'd tried to beg off, hadn't she? She tried asking them nicely and she'd tried demanding them to leave it be. But nooo, that little group of happy do-gooders just closed their ears as though she'd said nothing and gone on with their plans.

It was past time for talking, Sheri realized. It was time for action, and she was all over that like a bee to a honeycomb. It would be a much-needed distraction for her while providing a greatly-needed service for the small group of happy singles of Mule Hollow.

All she had to do now was find exactly the right man for the job.

That's right. She needed a man, and not just any man. She needed a man with as little desire for marriage as she had. She thought about her idea for a moment, letting it settle in and get comfortable. She would do this.

She certainly would.

She would find the perfect man to help with her little charade—a man whose name was not Simon Putts. No, this would be a man the ladies could picture Sheri with. He must be a man who valued his freedom and his freedom of choice with as much regard as she did.

All she needed to do now was figure out which of the cowboys in Mule Hollow would fit that specification. The two of them could teach the posse that when it came to running her life, Sheri was the one in control.

And she wasn't giving that up for anyone.

Ever.

Pace Gentry watched the scenery pass as he drove the last leg of the trip from Idaho to Texas. He'd crossed the border a couple of hours back and should have been feeling his mood brighten. After all, the long drive would come to an end within the hour. But it wasn't that simple. The end of the drive would also mark the end of the only life he'd ever known. The only life he'd ever wanted. And with that in mind, his mood had slipped lower with each passing mile.

Until a short few months ago when he'd realized God had different plans for him, he'd been about as content with his life as a man could be. He lived a simple life, for the most part alone but free on some of the most beautiful, untouched land God ever created. But that part of his life was done.

He blamed his surly mood on the fact that he was road weary. But he knew that wasn't it.

He'd signed on for this new life. He'd trusted the Lord to lead the way, to open doors that would put him where he was supposed to be. But in order to live life on God's terms he'd had to give up a simple life that hadn't ever required him to step too far out of his comfort zone.

That was about to change.

And truth be told, that made him uneasy.

Sheri changed into her running clothes the moment she got home from work. She needed a run in the worst way. More than the run, she needed to vent.

"Boy, did she ever need to vent," she mumbled, yanking the lace of her running shoe into a tight bow, then attacking the other one just as violently.

If she'd thought walking out of Sam's was going to deter the posse, she'd been oh so wrong. Those ladies were nothing if not tenacious. That's right, they'd just followed her down to the salon she and Lacy owned and spent the rest of the afternoon badgering her. It had taken everything she had to ward them off. Did they care that she was elbow-deep in pedicure water and didn't have time to be dealing with them?

Nope, they could have cared less. They were truly out of control. Rolling downhill and picking up speed in their attempt to manipulate her life.

They'd continued to ignore her every word of protest. Oh, it was enough to make a girl pull her hair out! Sheri yanked the shoelace instead, then stomped her foot for good measure. Couldn't they understand that just because her former boyfriend, J.P., had fallen in love with someone else, that didn't mean her heart had gotten stomped in the process? She was just fine.

Really, it wasn't a lie.

Well, not exactly. Yes, it hurt, much more than she wanted to admit. But Sheri wasn't about to throw fuel on that little secret fire.

No. They didn't need to know that for the first time in her life she'd thought she might be in love. *Might* being the operative word.

At first she told herself her heart was just aching because her pride had taken a kick in the gut. After all, she'd dared to open up to J.P. more than anyone before him. She'd even been on the verge of telling him she *might be* open to the idea of marriage. *Might be, even almost on the verge of,* was a major, major breakthrough for her. In all of her twenty-six years, she'd never before thought she'd make such an *almost* commitment. J.P. understood her feelings completely. They'd both had their reasons to shy away from commitment.

Poor J.P.

It wasn't as if he'd been planning to fall in love, either. He'd been blindsided by it just as much as she'd been.

Still, it had happened. Everyone who'd been at that wedding reception saw that love at first sight had struck him like a bolt of lightning. Only it wasn't with Sheri.

Sheri still felt slightly light-headed thinking about it. They'd been attending a wedding reception together, and she'd asked J.P. to get her a cup of punch. Just an innocent cup of punch. He'd been his sweet self, strutting off toward the punch bowl. *Bam!* Just like that, it had happened.

Love at the punch bowl.

Bizarre but true. Tara, the bride's friend from Houston, had come up for the wedding and was serving punch. When Tara and J.P. locked eyes with each other, that was it. They were goners.

"Goners for sure," Applegate Thornton had put it.

It was old news now. Really, really old news. It had been two months ago that the bolt of lightning had struck. However, their wedding had been yesterday, and instead of closing the book on *Poor Little Jilted Sheri*, it had only amplified the matchmaking posse's pity party for her. Actually, the entire town still felt sorry for her. Why, old Applegate and Stanley Orr were even giving her the sorrowful eye this morning.

Mule Hollow's resident grumpy old men, Applegate and Stanley, played checkers at the table by the front window of Sam's diner most mornings and lately some afternoons. When they looked at her as if she was some poor pathetic soul, it was almost more than she could take.

What was wrong with being a single gal, a *happy* single gal, thank you very much? Why were married women and old men convinced that marriage was the only way to happiness? She'd lived through more than her share of marriages with her parents. Nine, to be exact, and none of *them* had led to happiness.

As her mother was always saying, "Some people just aren't good at being tied down." How many times had Sheri heard that phrase? It was so true. Before J.P., she'd always grown bored and moved on after a few months. Sheri recognized that she was like her parents. This sudden ache in her heart only meant that she'd foolishly thought she might want more. That she'd changed, that her past didn't matter... She'd prayed about it a few times even though she hadn't expected an answer. She'd realized early on in her life that God spoke to some and she wasn't one of them. She hadn't let it get to her before, but lately that, too, was starting to bother her more and more.

As her footsteps pounded on the gravel road, Sheri felt as if she could burst with frustration. There had been times over the last two months jogging down this road that she had wanted to scream at the top of her lungs. She'd actually done it a couple of times—almost scared the cows to death. Still, there had been a certain freedom in letting loose.

As she rounded the bend in the road her mind locked on the matchmaking posse's unwanted plans for her life. Now, she thought with a grunt, might be a really good time to feel some of that freedom.

She opened her mouth to let a holler rip—and thankfully, spotted the truck before she screamed and embarrassed herself.

She slowed her pace. The dusty truck was parked off the road between the ancient roping pen and the shack that had always reminded her of something the first settlers had built when they'd come to the West. She slowed more, her gaze locking on the cowboy standing at the tailgate. She was more than glad she hadn't screamed. By the looks of this cowboy, if she'd startled him he'd probably have come running, guns ablaze. Of course, on closer inspection he wasn't wearing a holster, but that didn't take anything away from the impression he made.

She squinted but didn't recognize him. She headed his way. It never hurt to keep tabs on who was out here in the boonies of Mule Hollow.

He was unloading gear from the back of his truck, which was odd given that this was an access road to the interior of Lacy and her husband Clint's ranch. Lacy hadn't mentioned to her that anyone was moving in.

Actually relieved to have something new to take her mind off her own dilemma, Sheri jogged up the drive.

"So, how's it going, cowboy?" she called before she reached him. "Looks like you're moving in." She came to a halt a few feet behind him and placed her hands on her hips, awaiting a reply. None came.

Instead, as if he hadn't heard her, he reached for a coil of rope that lay on the tailgate beside a duffel bag and saddle. He slid the rope to his shoulder, then finally turned toward her.

If she'd been wearing four-inch heels, she'd have fallen straight off them. The man was gorgeous! The rugged, black-haired cowboy cocked his head toward her and met her startled gaze straight on with eyes the color of a stormy night sky.

Oh, my, my, my, looking at this handsome stranger confirmed what she'd known all her life. What she was trying to get the posse to realize about her.

She was not marriage material.

And that was *not* with a capital *N*.

Honestly, if all it took was one look into some stranger's eyes to remind her of the main reason she didn't make commitments—then there ya go. It was a done deal.

As her mom always said, *"Some people just aren't good at being tied down"*—but it wasn't only the echo of her mom.

Sheri just liked dating. There, her secret was out.

This was exactly the reminder she needed that the matchmakers were on a mission that would ultimately fail. And why she shouldn't feel bummed about it because really she enjoyed dating. She absolutely loved this. There simply wasn't anything as exciting as the initial spark of interest between a man and a woman. Like now, it was breathtaking. Then again, Sheri realized suddenly that the cowboy seemed to be breathing just fine.

Sheri reined in her runaway exhilaration and put her feet back on the ground. Her reaction to this handsome stranger had been so strong that it took a second to see that he didn't appear to have been bitten by the same bug.

Drat.

Instead, his steel-gray eyes skimmed over her with

disdain—as if he were looking at the latest order of pesticide.

Sheri's eyes widened as he adjusted the rope on his shoulder, then without uttering a word slung the saddle to his back and strode away.

Sheri realized suddenly that a little caution mighta been in order.

She hadn't lived in the city in a while, and obviously her guard was down. His cold look yanked her straight out of her imaginings and slam-dunked her right back into reality. She was standing in the middle of nowhere, alone, with a man who looked as though he could stare down a wildcat and never blink.

Who was she kidding? He looked as though he could shoot it, skin it and eat it for supper. Raw!

At last, she reacted like a smart woman and took a step back. But that dismissive glance…it bothered her. Sheri had come a long way from being the once shy little girl who expected to be ignored, so this just didn't sit well with her.

Oh yeah, baby. Danger or no danger, Sheri Marsh refused to be ignored by anybody, anywhere, anytime. She could excuse a guy for almost anything, even for falling in love with someone else, but she *would not* excuse a guy for ignoring her. Her hard-won "I'm here, I matter" personality demanded more.

"Hey, cowboy," she snapped and glared at his back. "I don't know where you come from, but around here cowboys have manners. When someone speaks, an answer is generally appropriate."

That got his attention, and he glanced over his

shoulder at her. She met his stare with her own. That's right, locked her spine, threw her shoulders back and dared him to ignore her again.

"Pace Gentry," he said without halting. "Not that it's any of your business."

Okay, as if that made her feel any better. Sheri's eyes narrowed to slits. The man hadn't even broken step as he disappeared inside the shack. Of all the unmitigated gall. She felt like the lid of a pressure cooker barely hanging on as she waited for him to reappear.

In an instant he returned and strode back to his truck…swaggered was more like it. Passed her by without so much as a glance. It struck her then that this wasn't any kind of cowboy she'd ever encountered. He was different in actions and in dress. It was subtle, but there were distinct differences.

Besides his collar-length hair, he had a strong jawline shadowed by a flat-rimmed, black Stetson devoid of the more traditional crease. Around his neck he wore a large checked bandanna tied loosely, as if he might pull it up at any moment to protect him from the trail dust of a hard cattle drive—

Or, with the dangerous glint in his eyes, maybe to rob a bank!

Then there were the spurs sticking out from beneath his chaps. They were more ornate than any Sheri had seen on the cowboys around Mule Hollow. These spurs were either for show or for intense business. From the look on his face, Sheri couldn't envision anything about him being for show.

Nope, this man was all business, easily mistaken for

a cowboy fresh off the trail a hundred years ago. Still, it was his intense gray eyes that told the story…this cowboy was one hundred percent authentic you-don't-want-to-mess-with-me cowboy.

Again, good sense mandated she turn around and get out of there immediately.

Yeah, right!

"Look, this is my friend's property, and I'm just making sure they know you're setting up camp out here."

She felt a sense of achievement when he stopped mid-swagger to glare at her. Suddenly, it felt as though he'd just weighed and measured her, and she'd come up lacking.

"Like I said," he drawled, his eyes cool. "Not that it's any more your business now than two minutes ago, but Clint knows I'm here."

The gravel in his drawl sent a shiver up Sheri's spine that had nothing to do with fright. "Lacy would have told me if someone was moving onto the ranch around the bend from me."

Hoisting a duffel bag to his shoulder he slammed the tailgate closed. His spurs sang a little ditty with every step he took away from her.

He'd dismissed her again!

"Hey, mister, the macho man thing's not really working for me."

He scowled down at her from the rickety porch. "Look, lady, I'm here to break horses. If you've got a problem with that, then take it up with Clint Matlock."

Before she could react, he disappeared into the tiny cabin and closed the door. Slammed the door was more like it. In her face, practically.

"Of all the rude, unmannered—" She halted mid-rant. He was probably inside the cabin watching through the window. No doubt laughing at the sight she must make standing in the middle of his drive with her mouth hanging open, her fists clinched at her sides. If only she had a mirror; she was no doubt fire-engine red with indignation.

The worst part about the entire situation was he was right. Boy, did that ever just annoy the thunder out of her. Well, not exactly right, she consoled herself. Fact was Clint and Lacy were her friends and she'd just wanted to make certain no funny business was going on out here on their property.

But since this Neanderthal was actually here for a reason then she had no right to continue questioning him. Spinning on her running shoes she raked a hand through her ponytail then jogged back to the road and headed home.

She'd only just begun her run, but she suddenly wasn't in the mood for jogging. Nope. She was in the mood to make a phone call and find out why Lacy hadn't seen fit to let her know she was about to have a neighbor.

If *neighbor* was what you could call the fierce-looking man she'd just met.

Chapter Two

Pace Gentry placed a few more pieces of wood on the campfire and watched the embers flutter as he settled into his bedroll for the night. Clasping his hands over his chest he relaxed and gazed up at the canopy of stars glittering above him. He could have slept inside the cabin, but tonight he needed to be outdoors.

He needed the connection to what he'd left behind.

He needed to feel the breeze whispering across the pastures to the north of him, hear the lonesome song of the coyotes and the occasional bawling of the cattle that grazed in the dark pastures surrounding him.

The sounds that made him feel at home.

The sounds that made him think for a moment he was back in the Great Basin, lost in the high desert of the Idaho range. Alone, with nothing but himself, God, his herd…

And his horses.

He loved his horses. It was in his blood. Nothing would make him happier than to die an old man as his dad had, atop a good ride. His dad had lived and died on his terms. Like his father, Pace understood bronc breaking was a tough way to make a living. He'd chosen it anyway.

Lived and breathed it.

With his dad's nomadic way of living, Pace hadn't ever really known any other life, but it hadn't mattered. Even if he'd turned out to be the worst cowboy around, he figured he'd have found a way to keep at it.

Pace watched a shooting star travel across the sky— something he'd have missed if he'd been inside. The howl of the coyote rippled into a full-blown serenade. Pace was forever grateful for the life he lived. Or had lived, he reminded himself, his gut shifting momentarily with doubt. He was on a new path. Like a surly bronc, for the first time in his life he felt the bit in his mouth and was fighting hard to get used to the feel of it.

If his earlier encounter was a measuring stick of how his transition was going to go…things weren't looking so good. Pace was the first to admit that he had some rough edges. Animals he could deal with, but people— he had little patience with interfering people. Meeting his pushy neighbor had proven those edges hadn't smoothed out on the long haul from Idaho to Texas.

He'd been his usual blunt self, a reaction he was going to be hard put to change.

Pulling his Stetson down over his eyes, he crossed his booted feet and settled in for the night. He figured the Lord had his work cut out for Him when it came to smoothing this rover's edges. But then, God was God, and if He could create the universe Pace figured, He could whip an ornery two-bit buckaroo into shape, too.

Pace just had a streak of buck left in him, and like the mustangs he was about to tame, that natural wildness was an instinct strong and deep in his soul.

Despite Pace's new commitment to change, more than likely this transition promised to be a rough ride.

"Rise and shine, Sheri," Lacy sang. "The mustangs are coming!"

Sheri bolted up from a dead sleep and squinted at the figure of Lacy standing in the stark light she'd flicked on as a wake-up call. Blinking and having murderous thoughts she peered at the red lights of her alarm clock. "Lacy! It's five o'clock in the morning. Are you *insane?*"

"Aww, now don't be that way," Lacy laughed.

Slamming her eyes shut, Sheri plopped back onto the bed with a thud and covered her face with her pillow. She didn't *do* early morning…and predawn—well, that wasn't even a time frame she acknowledged.

A fact Lacy was well aware of, but obviously ignored.

"C'mon, girlfriend. Up and at 'em. The mustangs are coming, and I want you to be there when they arrive. Here we go—"

Sheri yelped when her pillow and covers were abruptly yanked away, leaving no barrier against the hundred-watt bulb glaring at her from above. She needed to change that light, pronto.

Like a turtle without a shell, Sheri glared accusingly up at Lacy. Her pale blond hair stuck out from beneath her orange ball cap like pie meringue gone bad. A picture Sheri could easily visualize since right then and there she would love nothing more than to splatter a cream pie right smack in the dead center of her beaming face.

Of course, she wouldn't. "It's too early," she groaned instead.

"Get out of that bed, woman!"

Okay, maybe she would like to toss a pie, she thought, popping an eye open, watching Lacy drop the covers to the floor. When Lacy spun and reached for her hand, Sheri scowled at her as the fluffy cream pie sailed across her mind's eye.

"C'mon, Lacy, give a girl a break," she groaned again but couldn't help chuckling at the look Lacy gave her. The I've-heard-that-before look.

Nowadays, no one would realize that Sheri had been an extremely shy child until Lacy had befriended her. After being tugged along on Lacy's escapades, Sheri, the shy girl who'd learned to blend into the wall and not be seen, had slowly come out of her shell. It had totally been an act of survival.

But there were times, like now, that Sheri had to remind herself how grateful she was that Lacy had come along and changed her life for the better. Sheri dug her feet in at the bathroom doorway and stared at Lacy. "You know, I'm going to get you for this," she yawned.

"Trust me, Sheri. I have a hunch you're going to thank me once you down some coffee and see exactly what's waiting at the horse pens. Now get on in there, and I'll have you some coffee made when you get out. But you have to hurry, hurry, hurry!"

Before Sheri could make a comeback, Lacy gave one

last shove and yanked the door closed between them. "Just think, Sheri. Wild mustangs! Real, live American heritage at our ranch. It's the coolest thing."

"Yippy yiyay and yada, yada, yada," Sheri said softly as Lacy's chattering and the clunk of her boots retreated across the hardwood floor.

Peace and quiet at last. Sheri sighed. Slumping against the door, she raked her fingers through her hair, yawned, and thought about coffee.

Lacy made good coffee....

After a quick shower, she headed toward the kitchen feeling a bit more human. Although she wasn't sure she looked more human. For the sake of time and the early hour, she'd opted to yank her hair into a ponytail and slap her pink ball cap over it. And forget makeup. She and Lacy would just be a mess together, because no matter what—it was way too early in the morning to worry about appearances.

"Okay, girlfriend," she said, entering the kitchen. "Why did you drive all the way over here to wake me up and drag me all the way back over to your ranch? Especially when you know how grumpy I am at this hour." She latched on to the steaming mug Lacy held out to her, held it beneath her nose and let the rich aroma seep into her senses.

"Because with all the talk focused on you and J.P., I didn't have a chance to tell you about Pace and the horses. They're going to be in the pens around the corner from your house."

Sheri took a sip of coffee, only to wince at the reminder of the cowboy. "Speaking of which, I tried to call you about that last night. How could you not tell me someone was moving in over there? Is that place even fit for someone to move into?"

"Hey, I was goin' to tell you."

"*Goin' to* don't cut the mustard, sister."

Lacy made a face at her. "I can't help it. The girls came in and started up about all that J.P. business, and I couldn't get a word in edgewise. I did tell you that Clint's friend was moving to town to start a horse-breaking business. It was a while back, though, and believe me, from what Clint says that shack is a palace compared to what Pace was used to living in back in Idaho. Why, the man practically lived like a caveman."

"*That* I would believe."

Lacy smiled. "You met him, huh?"

Sheri did not smile. "Affirmative. The guy is definitely a Neanderthal. He's like, like…angry."

"He's not angry."

"So says you. The man is a grizzly. An angry grizzly."

"Sheri, he's just used to being alone. And he, well, he is here under duress, but he's willing, so he's not angry. He's just a fish out of water, so to speak."

"Maybe a barracuda." Sheri took another drink of coffee, ignoring the memory of those serious gray eyes.

"But he's cute, huh?"

Sheri rolled her eyes as she headed toward the door.

"Come on. Admit it, Sheri girl. He's, like, a hunk, and since when have you not noticed a hunk within a ten-mile radius?"

Since I very nearly got my heart trampled, that's when.

Sheri pushed away the thought and walked out onto

her porch, shocked all over again by the darkness and the fact that it was, by all appearances, still snoozing time. "Lacy, we're up before the roosters. Do you realize that?"

"Hey, it's good for you."

"*Hay* is for cows. And daybreak is for roosters," Sheri grumbled, opening the passenger door of Lacy's beloved 1958 pink Caddy. Not wanting to lose a precious drop of her coffee, she waited while Lacy sprang over to the driver's door in her usual Bo Duke style. Once she'd landed with a happy thud, then and only then did Sheri sit down beside her—a routine learned after many cups of sloshed coffee and speckled shirts.

"I can't believe you're trying to deny Pace Gentry is a hunk," Lacy continued as she backed the big car around and headed out of the driveway.

Sheri had learned over the years that it was best to keep some things to herself, or she would hang herself with incriminating evidence. With the matchmakers on red alert, now was not the time to admit that, despite his lack of manners, Pace *Neanderthal* Gentry was about the hunkiest hunk she'd ever seen. Even if that did sound childish and immature, it was the truth.

A thin, glowing line marked the horizon as they raced the hundred yards down the gravel road and around the corner to the cattle pens. She realized she'd been sleeping like a rock earlier because she hadn't heard any trucks passing by her house, and there had obviously been a parade of them.

There were cowboys milling around all over the place as Lacy guided the big car over every rut she could find. Grinning mischievously, she watched Sheri fight to keep her coffee in her cup.

Sheri chuckled. "Like I said earlier, I'm going to get you back for this. You know that, don't you?"

"Wouldn't be fun if you didn't. At least you're looking a little perkier."

"Thanks to the coffee, I might make it," Sheri said as the car came to a jolting halt.

"Hey, Sheri," several cowboys shouted in greeting as she slammed the car door shut.

"Mornin', boys," she called while waving, always happy to acknowledge a good-natured cowboy, even if the posse had practically put a Husband Wanted poster out on her behalf.

"How many horses are coming?" she asked, her gaze snagging on the one cowboy who might be a hunk, but could never in a million years be classified as a good-natured anything. He was standing beside the wooden corral talking to Clint. Grudgingly, Sheri admired them. Together they made a formidable picture of pure strength and manliness. Both were well over six feet, lean at the hips, wide at the shoulders. Extraordinarily handsome. But it was Pace her eyes fixed on, noting his steely gaze following her as she moved to stand beside Lacy. Sheri had to admit, she hadn't ever seen a better-looking man. But there was more to a good man than his looks, and this one—well, something was missing in the good-man category. That was for sure.

This morning he had on jeans and shorter chaps that came just below the knees with a wide band of fringe and silver conchos running up the sides. Oddly,

Sheri thought they were cute. They added a little flash to his otherwise rugged outfit. Feeling defiant, she lifted her hand and wiggled her fingers at him. He might have dismissed her the day before, but he had another think coming if he thought slamming a door on her meant she was done.

He tilted his head, acknowledging her wave, but that was it. There was no smile. Not that she'd expected one, but there was not even a hint of a change in Pace's facial expression. What was his problem? The man was certainly peculiar.

"Clint said about twelve mustangs," Lacy was saying. "You can only adopt four mustangs a year but Clint and Pace got special permission from the Bureau of Land Management to get a few extra, though they won't get papers on all of them this year. The government is very protective of the mustangs. Pace has plenty of horses to train. People are lining up waiting on him to work with their horses because he's so good. Sheri, are you listening to me?"

"Ah—yes, sure." She yanked her gaze away from Pace, hoping Lacy hadn't noticed her staring at him. Then she wondered why she cared. She could stare if she wanted to.

The distinct sound of an 18-wheeler could be heard growling around the bend. Lacy, along with everyone else, turned toward the sound.

"Speaking of Pace, what's this guy's full story?" Sheri asked. Her gaze skipped back to the cowboy who was now watching the truck's approach. Despite his bad manners there was no denying that he intrigued her.

When she looked back toward the truck, she met Lacy's gaze. Drat, she'd been caught. The last thing she needed was Lacy getting any ideas. But Lacy wasn't smiling. Instead, a thoughtful gleam shone in her eyes.

"I don't really know much," Lacy said, shaking off her serious look, "except what I already told you. How he lived in that cabin in Idaho alone for months is a mystery to me. I'd climb the walls. Can you imagine—no telephone, or water? He washes his clothes in the nearby river. The ice-encrusted river. He's really like a mountain man. But we're talking huge ranches here. Like five hundred square miles or more, not acres. Miles of barren, lonesome land. That's why he lived in the little shack like that. They need men spread out watching over smaller sections over the winters. Even in the summers he doesn't see much more than a handful of people. Not me, I couldn't handle that. I've got to talk to people."

Sheri knew that was right. She could live alone much easier than Lacy. Lacy would talk the bark off a tree if she didn't have people around to absorb her chatter. If Lacy were to live like Pace—oh, boy, the cows snowed in with her alone over a long winter would probably know the English language come springtime. Sheri smiled thinking about it.

The big truck and its huge trailer pulled to a halt, the sound drowning out their voices; Sheri leaned in close so Lacy could hear her question. "So he's going to lease the land and break horses?" She was curious. She told herself it was only because he was going to be living beside her. But she knew it was because, despite everything, there was something about the guy that she found appealing.

Lacy nudged her in the ribs, and Sheri realized she'd been staring at Pace again. So shoot her, she liked to look at him. Not only was he easy on the eyes, but also his stance was that of a man who was very comfortable in his skin. That was a major attraction to Sheri.

"It's like this, Sheri. Clint says Pace is one of the best there is at breaking horses. So when he called Clint and said he'd decided to go into business for himself but needed a place to start, Clint jumped at the chance to get him to Mule Hollow. He offered the lease in trade for Pace breaking some colts for him. They've worked something out. Plus, according to Clint, they go way back. His dad used to break horses some summers for Clint's dad."

Sheri found herself watching Pace again; she couldn't help herself. He strode across the lot to the big truck, his hat was pulled low over his eyes, and there was this little hitch in his stride that made the fringe of his chaps dance and the spurs on his boots sing.

Okay, so the man was fascinating.

So was a porcupine. Both could sting a person if they weren't careful.

The horses in the huge trailer were whinnying and cutting up something fierce. Sheri wasn't thinking about the mustangs, however, as Pace untied his horse from the trailer and stepped up into the stirrup. In one graceful move, he was seated in the saddle.

Sheri lost her breath at the sight. It just whooshed right out of her. If ever there was a man meant for the saddle, it was this one. Wow. Tall and straight as a rod, he sat with a command that took Sheri straight back to the heroes of the Old West. She just couldn't shake that image of him. She swallowed and fought off the sigh that tried to escape her lips. *Get a grip, girl.*

"Come on, Sheri, let's get up to the fence so we can watch them unload."

"Um, right," she said, blinking. Following Lacy to the corral, she climbed up onto the second rung and hung on to the top board with one hand. She drank the last of her now-cold coffee as she watched the action.

The air crackled with energy as Pace rode his horse into the corral, then moved to the side as the truck doors were pulled open. When the first black mustang exploded into the pen, Sheri was immediately struck by what she was seeing. This was a part of history. Majestic and wild the proud horses galloped out of the interior of the transport trailer. Heads held high and manes flying, the horses were utterly beautiful as they trotted down the ramp and loped around the circle of the large pen. It was awesome. *Awesome!*

"Pace, he's going to break these horses?" she gasped. Suddenly, it seemed a shame to tame something so untouched. The word *break* just held a connotation that seemed almost criminal when used in reference to these proud animals. They were supposed to be wild and free—

"Clint says no one can do what Pace can do. He's the best there is at giving a horse manners while still letting it retain its dignity and character."

"So that's his excuse," she said softly.

"What's does that mean?" Lacy asked, looking at her funny. Only then did Sheri realize she'd spoken out loud.

She smiled. "He's been reading the wrong book."

"Huh?"

Sheri laughed. "From the way he was acting yesterday it's obvious that Cowboy Pace has been spending too much time reading the book on horse manners and hasn't even cracked open the one on cowboy manners."

Lacy looked from her to Pace and back again, a sparkle in her eye. "Well, Sheri, maybe he needs someone to open the book for him."

"Oh, no, you don't." Sheri stepped down from the fence shaking her head. "I know trouble when I see it. That man might be easy on the eyes, but he's a heartbreaker."

Lacy followed her as she walked away from the pen. "I don't think so."

"Come on, Lacy, it's written all over him. That guy would shy away from commitment quicker than…" Sheri paused and thought about what she'd just said.

"You?" Lacy finished, grinning as if she'd just won the cow chip toss. *She always won the cow chip toss.*

"Yeah," Sheri admitted, turning back to look at her neighbor with an entirely new perspective.

Sheri wasn't one to think that the Lord paid much attention to her needs. In all fairness, she'd stopped trying to get any special attention from Him a long time ago. Lacy was the one with the direct line to Him. For years Sheri had coasted on her coattails when it came to all that. She'd be lying if she didn't admit that it bothered her some. Maybe at one point a lot. But it wasn't as if she was going to beg anybody for attention and certainly not God.

Anyway, she understood that when it came to trying

to please the Lord, Lacy had that wrapped up. Lacy lived to please Him, and Sheri couldn't really blame the Lord for giving Lacy more attention. Sheri loved Lacy like a sister and knew she could never have the heart that Lacy had. Why pretend? Some people were good enough to have priority in the Lord's eyes, and some weren't. No matter what people might say, that was the way it worked.

Still, *if* she'd said a prayer for the Lord to send her someone to get the posse off her back—well, she figured Pace Gentry might be the answer to that prayer.

But since she hadn't asked the Lord for His help and Pace had turned up anyway, she knew it was only a co-incidence. Still, she was no dummy. She wouldn't throw away a golden opportunity when it rode right up to her. Look out, Mule Hollow Matchmakers, the game was on.

Chapter Three

Pace looked over each mustang, assessing them as he guided his mare through their ranks. They looked healthy despite the long trip from the Oklahoma Field Station. A bit ragged, but healthy. They were scared and wary though, congregating in a tight knot and moving about the pen as one unit.

Because they'd made such a long trip and now were in unfamiliar territory, he wanted to make certain their transition was as easy as possible. His own transition gave him even more empathy for these poor creatures. He herded the first six into the second pen then waited on the next group to be released from the second compartment of the trailer. Once he was satisfied that they, too, had made the trip without being injured in the crowded trailer, he rode to the gate and nodded at the young cowhand to let him pass.

"Mr. Gentry," he said as Pace rode his horse through the gate he held open. "I'd like to come out and watch you work if you'd let me. I mean, sir, Clint said he'd let me help you anytime you needed help."

Pace dismounted and studied the younger man. He recognized the familiar light in his eyes. "You can come out some—we'll see about helping me. First, you have to call me Pace. My dad was Mr. Gentry. What's your name?" Pace held out his hand.

"Jake, sir."

He accepted Pace's handshake, and Pace noticed with satisfaction that he had an easy but firm grip. That went a long way in handling a scared horse. "You want to break horses?"

"If I can do it your way, sir. I've broke a few, gentled some, but frankly, sir, when I saw that documentary you were featured in I knew I didn't really have a clue how to do it the right way."

"Do you have patience?"

"Um, yes, sir. I do."

Pace nodded. "Come out the end of next week. Right now I want some time alone with them. They need time to adjust to the trip and the change of scenery."

Jake grinned and nodded as though he'd just been given the best present under the Christmas tree. "Yes, sir. I'll be here. You need anything else, you call me. I'm at Clint's bunkhouse."

Pace watched the younger man leave, reminded of himself, recognizing the gleam in his eyes.

"Hello, neighbor. What's that you said about patience?"

Pace twisted around, recognizing the voice he knew belonged to his nosy, beautiful neighbor. He might have been less than friendly the day before, but that didn't mean he hadn't noticed her. He'd noticed plenty.

He'd been watching her ever since she'd climbed out of that atrocious car of Lacy's.

He studied her, taking his time, thinking if he could keep her offended enough, maybe she'd leave him alone…. She was staring at him with a playful smirk on her lips that matched the easy lilt of her voice. A tone very different from the irritated one of the day before. Today, she had a bright hat on that said Mornings and Hair Don't Mix, and she was right. Her chestnut, shoulder-length hair was more out of her ponytail than in. It reminded him of a horse's tail that had tangoed with a crop of scrub bushes.

"My name's Sheri Marsh, by the way. Thought I'd tell you since you had that sudden emergency inside your cabin yesterday and didn't have time to inquire."

There was mischief in her eyes as she held her hand out to him. She had long, slender fingers, and he hesitated before reluctantly wrapping his callused fingers around hers. He swallowed hard at her touch, feeling an unexpected connection as her soft hand met his.

"Patience with people—" he started, his gaze meeting hers and suddenly his gut felt the way it did the moment before he settled into the saddle of a bronc "—is on an entirely different level for a loner like me," he finished, realizing only then that he was still hanging on to her hand. He dropped it like a hot branding iron, then reached to check the saddle cinch on his horse. His movements out of sync, he forced himself to focus on what he was doing instead of the woman standing near him.

Stepping closer, she ran her hand down the flank of his horse. "Believe me, I figured that one out myself," she said drily.

He shot her a sideways glance from beneath his Stetson. She was standing close enough that he caught the fresh scent of her. Something tangy and tart, like the personality that radiated from her.

"Well, anyway, cowboy. I just thought I'd tell you that I was sorry to interfere with your business yesterday. I was only looking out for Clint and Lacy."

He nodded and tried to work up the will to say he was sorry for his behavior. But before he could respond, she spun on her bright red city boots and strode away.

He didn't call her back, but watched her leave instead. She bounced as though she were walking on springs.

He realized suddenly that he wasn't alone in watching Sheri Marsh sashay away. Almost every cowboy in his line of vision and probably on the lot had stopped what they were doing and were calling goodbyes to his striking neighbor. She knew it, too. She tilted her head to this side, then that, smiling at each one and waving. The woman acted as if she were on the red carpet or something. There was no doubt that she was one hundred percent comfortable standing in the limelight. Again, that did not surprise him.

Pace had always liked Sam's Diner. It was a diner and pharmacy all rolled into one, like so many drugstores had been way back when. This one was complete with the original marble soda fountain and spinning bar stools. He could still remember the first time he walked into the place as a kid. He'd been ten, and he and his dad had been on the road for eighteen hours straight. Pace had been starving, and the smell of bacon and eggs had started his stomach growling the minute they'd walked through the heavy swinging door. Even as a kid he'd been taller than the bowlegged man who came storming from behind the counter and grabbed his dad's hand. He'd shaken it so hard it looked like a strong-arm contest.

Pace smiled at the memory of wiry little Sam taking on his six-foot-four-inch dad. To this day he'd never met anyone who could shake hands like Sam.

"How ya doing, son?" Sam greeted him heartily as he grabbed the hand Pace held out. Though Sam had aged, his grip had only grown stronger. Pace was pretty certain it came from years of practice on all the customers who walked through his doors. "Sorry to hear about yer dad," he said, pumping away. "It was a terrible shame. He was a good man."

"Thank you, sir. He died doing something he loved. He was luckier than most in that respect. I doubt he had any regrets when it came to the life he lived."

Sam let go of his hand at last, crossed his arms and nodded thoughtfully. "Yer right about that, son."

From the window table Pace heard a snort and glanced toward the two old-timers hunched over a game of checkers. Seemed nothing much changed around Mule Hollow.

"Sam'd be right smart if he took a lesson from yer daddy on that," Applegate Thornton practically shouted as his opponent, Stanley Orr, nodded.

It had been five years since Pace had traveled through Mule Hollow, and he wasn't sure if those two old-timers had moved an inch since he left.

"Turn yer hearin' aid on, App, yer shoutin' loud enough to wake the dead," Sam ordered, then turned back to Pace and Clint. "What kin I get fer you boys?"

It was early for lunch but late for breakfast so they settled on burgers with sautéed onions and fries. They'd chosen a booth near the back of the diner, one they'd huddled in on many occasions when they'd kicked around as early teens. If he wasn't missing Idaho so much, Pace would have felt as if he'd come home. But try as he might, he was still fighting a longing for what he'd left behind. He was trusting that the Lord was going to help handle that with time.

"How are you doing with the move?" Clint asked as if reading his thoughts.

Pace set his hat in the seat next to him, then met his old friend's knowing gaze. "I'd be lying if I said I wasn't having trouble. I keep asking myself what the Lord needs me for down here."

"Could be He just needs you to be willing to follow Him."

Pace hadn't thought about that. "Could be."

Clint clasped his hands on the table and leaned forward. "I think it's more than that. I believe you'll be surprised by God's plans for you. You're thinking he can't use you because you're not the most social guy I know. On that I have to agree, but he used silent types all through the Bible." Clint grinned. "The thing is, God doesn't need any of us. We need Him."

"Yeah, my dad said something similar right before he died." Pace felt the familiar tug on his heartstrings thinking about the last days with his dad. An extremely quiet man, he'd raised Pace all alone after his mother died giving birth to him. He'd taught Pace to be the man he'd become. He'd been overjoyed when Pace had finally come to love the Lord. Pace thanked God his dad lived long enough to see him accept Christ. It blessed Pace every time he remembered the hug his dad had wrapped him in when Pace told him.

"If only I'd inherited Dad's patience."

Clint laughed hard at that as Pace knew he would.

"If only, if only."

"I'm serious, Clint. Did I tell you how I just about bit the head off my new neighbor?"

"Sheri?" Clint's eyes widened. "All I can say is watch out. That gal can bite back."

"Tell me about it."

Sam came out carrying two large plates and a bottle of ketchup. He placed them on the table then turned to leave.

"Sam," Clint said, drawing him back. "Did you hear Adela's daughter is after her to move to Abilene?"

Sam stiffened.

"'A' course he heard," Stanley called.

"But do you think it's spurred him on to pop the question?" Applegate boomed. "Nope. He's still keepin' his lips buttoned up like an old fool."

An almost wistful look passed over Sam's face before he glared at his two friends. "Can't a proprietor get any peace in his own place of business? What happened to the two of you getting out of here by nine?"

"It's called re-tar-ment," Applegate snapped. "And it's fer the birds."

"Yeah," Stanley sighed. "These here golden years ain't exactly what we expected."

"Well, if that's why y'all keep stayin' in my business then I wish you'd go back to work," Sam growled.

"We're stayin' in yer business 'cause we're yer friends," Applegate snapped. "You love that sweet woman and need to ask her to marry ya, and I aim ta bother ya 'til ya do."

Sam grumbled his way back into the kitchen.

"What's up?"

Clint shrugged. "Honestly, we don't know. He's loved Adela forever. Her husband's been dead around sixteen years, but Sam won't ask her to marry him. Everyone knows if he did she'd say yes. It's baffling, especially because we know he wants to. But from what he's told a few of the guys over the past few months, he can't get over the fact that she loved her first husband so much."

"You think that's all there is to it?"

"I don't know, Pace, it just doesn't make sense. I think there's something more, but you know Sam. He won't talk unless he's good and ready."

Pace could relate to that.

"The only thing that worries me is if Adela were to leave, I think it would break his heart. He's been real moody for the last few months, and I think it's wearing on him. That, or something else is wrong with him and he's not letting on."

"Maybe you should talk to him."

"Don't think I haven't tried."

Pace was driving home an hour later and kept thinking about Sam. The man had lived basically seventy years a bachelor. Maybe he just couldn't see changing his situation after all this time. It seemed that the town had a preoccupation with weddings, and he could see why. He remembered the first time he and his dad lived here. That had been when the oil was flowing freely and there seemed to be as many oil wells dotting the pastures as mesquite trees. It took men to run the wells, and the town was busting at the seams with families. Not the case when they'd come the last time to break some horses for Clint's dad. The wells had been locked up and the families gone, leaving behind only the ranches and a town that seemed like a ghost of what it had been. He'd been eighteen, but he'd noticed it. It was nice to see it coming to life again.

He just had to hope nobody got any ideas about fixing him up. He drove past the little white house where his neighbor lived. The woman had all kinds of stuff in her yard. There were strange sparkling things hanging out of the trees, made from what looked like triangles cut from mirrors and copper sheeting. One large tree was so sparkly, it looked as if it had earrings on it. In the flower beds there were spikes of copper tubing and what looked to be cups and saucers stuck on top of them like whimsical bird feeders. Her yard seemed alive with sound and movement as the summer breeze wove its way through the obstacle course.

There were bright painted birdhouses along the fence line, and her mailbox was painted bright purple with yellow daisies all over it. Then there was an assortment of hummingbird feeders hanging from the porch.

He'd never seen anything like it. He shook his head and moved on past the house. The woman was either hobby crazy or spent all her money on flea market finds. Neither image fit the woman he'd met. Maybe all the stuff came with the house. That would seem more like it, since Sheri Marsh didn't appear the sort to tinker with yard decorations. Then again, she didn't seem the sort to tinker with flowers, either, and they were hanging off window boxes and overflowing from pots and beds. Even if those had come with the house she would have to tend them. She didn't seem to be a tender, a nurturer.

His conscience pricked. How would he know, really? He'd been rude to her yesterday, but she'd reared up at him like a mamma wildcat protecting her cubs and that hadn't set well with him.

He should apologize.

Moving on, he rounded the bend toward his place and the horses waiting there. The work, the familiar. He was not familiar with watching what he said. Back in Idaho there wouldn't be any need to watch his words or any need for apology. He'd have been alone out there, working with the horses and taking care of his cows. Out there in the wide-open space and endless plains, he wouldn't have to worry about neighbors popping in unannounced demanding things. It was a simpler life. The kind of life suited for a man like him—a man who'd been raised to live by his own rules....

What was he doing? Pace slammed on the brakes in

front of the horse pens. He was here to learn to live life by God's rules.

He hadn't come here to disappear. He hadn't come here to crave solitude and wish for things to go back to the way they'd been. But he did, and despite his determination to change, this longing for his old life wasn't easing up as the days passed. Especially with this building conflict with his neighbor.

Pace saddled his horse Yancy and rode out onto the open range. Clint's ranch was one of the largest in Texas, and back in the interior Pace could almost get the sense of the Great Basin. The terrain was sweeping and vast with hills and valleys rubbing up against rocks and ridges. It wasn't Idaho, but riding anywhere always helped him relax.

He was riding along the fence line, heading back toward his cabin, when he spotted Sheri jogging along the road. She was a long way from home and didn't look as though she was tiring at all. He had a feeling Sheri Marsh never tired out.

"Hey, cowboy," she called the minute she spotted him.

Fighting off the urge to turn Yancy around and gallop off, he watched her jog up to the fence separating them. Standing there grinning, the sassy woman made him figure that a man with any sense would heed the warning and run. But Sheri drew him in like the most ornery filly in a herd always did. He was a sucker for a good challenge, and challenge radiated off his neighbor like flames from a burning building.

"You don't talk much, do you?" she said.

"Always been a downfall of mine," he said, resting his hands on the saddle horn.

She kicked a rock, watched it skitter across the dirt. "I used to be that way."

His disbelief must have shown because her grin widened.

"It's true," she protested.

"I didn't say anything."

"Oh, yes you did. I heard you loud and clear."

"What happened?"

"Lacy Brown. Well, Matlock now. She just bullied the shyness out of me. Always dragging me around and forcing me to step up. She's a brute, that one."

"Did Clint know this before he married her?"

"Oh yeah. Believe me, he tried to fight it, but she's contagious. Thank goodness. Now, I kinda like speaking my mind and getting noticed."

"That's more than apparent."

They studied each other until she lifted her eyes to watch a blue jay chase a sparrow out of its territory. "Bully," she called as they zipped by, the sparrow doing evasive maneuvers, and the blue jay squawking in loud pursuit. Pace chuckled before he could stop himself.

She shot him an indignant look. "They are. They're always chasing something or griping about it."

"I didn't say anything."

"Yes, you did. Don't forget, I can hear you, Pace Gentry. So, is it true that you're the best there ever was at bustin' a bronc?"

"Well, I don't know about that. I can get the job done."

"Are you competing in the rodeo Mule Hollow is putting on at the end of the month?"

Behind him the sun emerged from a cloud and Sheri lifted a hand to shade her eyes, still squinting. She was cute, even with the awful-looking face she was making. It was easy to see why she was so popular with the cowboys.

"Are you?" he asked, causing her to double over with a laugh before springing back up, her eyes twinkling.

"Me?"

"Why's that so funny?"

"The only thing cowgirlish about me is my love of boots. I barely know which end of that horse you're on is which."

Pace's lip curved up on one side. "Yancy might take that as an insult." He liked the way her eyes lit up mischievously. "So you live in cattle country, but you're not a cowgirl?"

She gave a one-sided grin. "That'd be right, bud. I jog on my own two feet. I tried a horse once and fell off."

"Were you wearing those red frog giggers?"

"Frog giggers! What's a frog gigger? Are you callin' my boots ugly?"

"If the shoe fits…"

She slapped her hand to her hip. "Hey, you better back up now. Calling a woman's footwear ugly is almost as bad as telling her she has an ugly baby."

"Wouldn't want to do that." He couldn't help his grin now. He'd smiled more in the last ten minutes than he'd smiled since making the decision to leave Idaho.

"Smart man."

Not so much, he decided, realizing he was enjoying

her spunk just a little too much. He straightened in the saddle and pulled his head out of the clouds. "Well, I need to get back to work." He tipped his hat and nudged Yancy forward, more than aware that she was surprised by his sudden departure.

He could feel her eyes on his back watching him leave. He didn't look back. The last thing he needed was to get ideas about his neighbor. He didn't need female complications thrown in on top of trying to build a business and figuring out what God wanted from him.

Chapter Four

Well, so much for thinking they were making progress and having a decent conversation! The man had just closed up and rode off without so much as a *have a nice day.*

"Hey, cowboy," Sheri called after Pace. When he didn't bother to glance back at her despite the almost-pleasant conversation they'd had, Sheri felt her face grow hot. "You are about the rudest man I've ever met," she shouted across the distance, making certain he heard her loud and clear.

He didn't nod his head, wave his hand or in any way acknowledge that she'd just insulted him. What a jerk.

Clamping her lips in a hard line, it took everything she had to hold back the smart crack begging to be let loose. Instead she forced herself to let him go as she resumed her jog. The man was impossible.

Maybe she needed to rethink involving Pace in her plan. Surely she could find someone else to fit the requirements. Even as she thought it she knew that—rude as he was—he was the right man for the job.

It was obvious the man would never marry—not with that mood disorder. Surely he wouldn't want the posse trying to fix him up, and that made him perfect.

Her conscience pricked thinking about it. All night long she'd told herself she had good reasons for trying to teach the ladies a lesson…but it was complicated and she wasn't certain even she could pull it off. She needed to believe in what she was going to do if she was going to be able to pull if off.

"I do believe," she said aloud.

She was no math whiz, but she could add—unlike the matchmakers. If the Lord had intended for everyone to get married, then the ratio of men to women would be equal. Right?

Right. It might sound silly, but after watching her parents marry—and divorce—as many people as they could, it fit. It was disgusting.

Sheri recognized the truth. Fear of following in her parents' footsteps factored heavily in her reasons for not wanting to fall in love. And with good reason, she rationalized. She grew bored too easily. No matter how wonderful the guy was, her restlessness always ruined it. Clearly a genetic trait, with her parents' history and all.

It didn't take an Einstein to figure out some people just weren't marriage material. She'd recognized the truth about herself long ago and made peace with it. She simply wanted to go back to the way it had been. She'd always had fun dating the guys she wanted to date then moving on when the time came. Her surprise almost-commitment to J.P. had been a huge step for her. Now she recognized that it had been brought on by the happily-ever-after atmosphere of Mule Hollow. It had invaded the water system, and it was in the air, too. Love. That had to be it. The love bug was floating around, and she'd caught it for a moment. That was the only excuse she could think of that would explain why she'd stepped over the line and found herself at the *almost*-commitment stage.

These feelings she was experiencing were a good lesson in why she'd been so cautious. Heartache. Not heartbreak, exactly, thank goodness. Still, she shouldn't have let her guard down. Really, from now on the joy she got from dating might be diminished for fear that she might be tempted to cross that line again. *Arrgggh!* It was frustrating. She was content with her life the way it was. She was.

And she would be again. There was life after J.P. She had her head on straight again, and she would choose not to ever live the way her parents had lived. She'd never bring a kid into a potential time bomb. That was her motivation, the fear that she had her parents' genes of discontent. Her mother's words rang through her head once more…. *Some people just aren't good at being tied down.* That might be true, but knowledge was power, and Sheri would use that power to control her life.

This sudden fascination with Pace so closely after thinking she might have been in love with J.P. was a sure sign of things to come. There was only one way for someone like herself to avoid a string of divorces: avoid marriage like the plague.

That was the reason she was going through with this plan.

The posse needed someone to show them that they should respect people's choices. It hurt too badly as a kid to be yanked from Mom's to Dad's and back again, and it hurt too much almost letting her heart think it could have the fairy-tale happy ending.

She was going to make the ladies realize that pushing a person into something that wasn't right for them could get a person hurt. Moody Pace Gentry was just the guy to help her.

That's right. Whirling around, she jogged after him. He was perfect for this, and she was going to convince him to help her. No more misgivings about it. This was the right thing to do.

Plan halfway in place, Sheri jogged up Pace's driveway and went in search of him. She found him behind the house inside a round pen that sat off by itself. It was lined with thin, split tree trunks.

Hearing the sound of Pace talking, she moved toward the structure, found a crack to peek through and made like a statue. Pace stood about thirty feet from her. He was standing in front of a chestnut-colored horse.

She hadn't meant to spy on the guy, but couldn't very well interrupt him now that she could see he was working. She also couldn't stop her curiosity from getting the better of her. She was interested in how he worked. He was, after all, supposed to be the best.

So there she stood, rooted to the crack in the fence, watching and listening as he talked softly to the wary animal. Despite his surly manners, she got a kick and a half out of looking at him, probably because he reminded her of the heroes from the movies she enjoyed watching. She was nuts about movies. Westerns in particular. Not that he looked like Gary Cooper or John Wayne, but somehow he possessed their essence....

Okay, her brain was gone. She was losing it, but she couldn't help herself. She remained quietly hidden, steadily watching.

In Pace's hand he held a coiled rope which he was rubbing down the torso of the horse as he spoke to it in a silky voice. She remembered this horse. It had raced off the truck first and stayed as far away from people as it could get. That Pace was able to get within ten feet of it surprised her. What a difference a few days could make. Or was it the difference Pace could make? He was so calm standing there letting the horse get used to him. The way she would treat a scared puppy.

Pace held the coil of rope up and let the horse see it. Then he touched the rope to the horse's neck, then its shoulder. She noticed that he used the coiled rope to push on the horse, too. She knew there was a reason behind every touch he administered.

His smooth as silk voice was so contrary to the gruffness he'd shown her that it startled her. Watching him in action, Sheri could totally believe he was the best. There was a gentleness she'd certainly never seen. Sheri watched for at least an hour. She couldn't help it. Time flew by. It was the most remarkable thing she had ever witnessed.

After a while, sanity returned, and she realized there wouldn't be an opportunity to talk without interrupting him. She finally backed away and walked down the driveway unnoticed. As she jogged her way around the bend toward home, she was filled with a quiet sense of awe.

It was a nice reprieve after all the turmoil she'd been experiencing.

Pace Gentry. What a contradiction. For as long as she lived, she didn't think she'd ever see anything more extraordinary than the look on his face as he worked with that horse.

It wasn't the tight scowl he wore outside the round pen. It was an expression of total contentment. He was at home within the boundaries of that circle. He was relaxed and in control. It was clear as day that Pace had been born a bronc buster.

She paused in her driveway and walked beside the sweet-scented honeysuckle vine that wound around her mailbox and ran down the length of the fence among her brightly colored birdhouses, her own mini Mule Hollow. She smiled, listening to her wind chimes singing softly in the breeze and studied her flowers as she passed.

What Pace did was lead the horses to an understanding. Exactly! His gift was that he worked with the animals until they chose to wear a saddle. He mesmerized them until they said, "Throw that saddle on up there and hop on, cowboy."

It seemed almost laughable, yet that was exactly what it looked like.

Now she knew his secret.

Pace Gentry was like a Dr. Dolittle when it came to

horses. He could practically talk to the animals. He just couldn't talk to people!

Or, he chose not to talk to people. Or maybe just not to her.

Hmm, the man was more perplexing and interesting than any man Sheri had ever encountered.

She kind of liked that.

The salon was busy the next day. Sheri had arrived at work distracted. She hadn't slept well the night before, and it was her neighbor's fault. Instead of sleeping she found herself thinking about what would make a man like him leave behind a life he loved. As she worked on Edith Musgroves's toes, she forced herself to focus on her reasons for wanting to acquire his help in executing her plan. They weren't personal, she reminded herself, this was business. She needed to keep that in mind. At any other time dating him for real would have been a done deal. She'd have been all about seeing what he was about.

But for the purpose of achieving her goal all these thoughts about Pace Gentry's personal life really needed to stay out of the mix. They could only complicate things. She'd chosen him because he fit the profile. He was a man who, like her, appreciated his freedom. It was obvious. Though she didn't have this on authority, from what she'd observed and what she'd heard of the man her assumptions made sense. Now all she had to do was convince him to help her.

As the day ended Lacy finished her haircuts first and headed home, leaving Sheri to close up shop. Intent on approaching her neighbor again, Sheri had just locked up and was climbing into her Jeep when an overall-clad Norma Sue came barreling across Main Street from Pete's Feed and Seed, holding on to her straw hat as she ran.

"Sheri, hold up there a minute," she called.

Sheri went ahead and climbed into her open-topped vehicle, noticing some jokester had used his finger to write the words *Wash me* in the dust-covered red paint. "Cute," she muttered, wondering which cowboy had left his mark as he'd passed by.

Dust in August was a way of life out here, especially when one lived on a dirt road as she did. Even so, she loved Texas in August. Sheri had always been infatuated with the outback of Australia, but she was afraid of heights and hated flying. Flying that far was out of the question, so the dry heat of western Texas in August was as close as she'd get to the real outback.

Enjoying the heat, she breathed in the dry air and watched Norma Sue hustle toward her, sweating as she came. Sheri got a picture in her head of the posse hog tying her and tossing her on the first plane to Australia in an attempt to fix another aspect of her life if they knew she had a fear of flying.

"Whew-ee! This heat is about to fry me whole," Norma Sue said, fanning herself with her hat as she slid to a halt beside Sheri. "I just wanted to invite you to church tomorrow. We've been missing you something fierce lately."

There you go, Sheri thought grudgingly. This was one more thing they were set on fixing about her.

"Norma Sue," she sighed, "we've been through this."

"Sheri, you haven't come to church since you and J.P. broke up. You can't take what happened out on the Lord."

Sheri was not taking it out on the Lord…well maybe a little. But that was between her and Him. It wasn't Norma Sue's concern that she'd had about all the secondhand blessings she could take. Still, she wasn't about to tell Norma Sue that she was feeling forgotten by God. It was childish but true, and Sheri honestly couldn't explain her feelings. She just knew that lately when Sunday morning rolled around she didn't have the desire to get up and go to church. After all, what had the Lord done for her lately?

It had become a subtle issue between her and Lacy, too, but Lacy had backed off, and Norma Sue and the posse were going to have to do the same. After having lived in Dallas for so long, Sheri was having trouble with the fact that in a small town like Mule Hollow everyone knew her business. If she missed church everyone knew it and thought their input was welcomed.

It wasn't that she didn't love the people of Mule Hollow. She did, but there were boundaries that needed to be established.

"I'll come when I'm ready, Norma Sue," she said firmly. "Right now, I'm not." Her conscience pricked her a bit as she heard her biting tone, but she was tired of this.

"Then how about coming to my house on Monday night for a little Bible study we're starting up?"

"I don't think so." Frustrated, Sheri turned the ignition and listened as the engine coughed then started up.

Norma Sue smacked her hat back onto her wiry, gray hair and placed both hands on her robust hips. "Then promise me you'll at least think about it."

Sheri slumped slightly, her hand tightening on the gearshift. "*Okay.* I'll promise you that, but I'm not promising you anything else."

Norma Sue smiled. "Fair enough."

Sheri backed the Jeep onto Main Street.

"I know your heart is broken, Sheri," Norma Sue called, "but God is on your side and so are we. You just give it some time and everything is going to work out fine."

Sheri refused to let her mouth drop open! Instead she rammed the gear into Drive and pressed the gas too hard. The Jeep shot down the street as though it were a race car doing zero to sixty in four seconds flat—all right, ten seconds....

Though four wouldn't have been fast enough to suit Sheri.

Knuckles white, hot wind in her hair, Sheri glanced at herself in the mirror. "Pace better get on board pretty quick—that's all I've got to say."

She was nervous thinking about it. Really, did she just go up and say, "Hey, I need you to pretend to be my boyfriend." No, too pathetic.

Besides that, he'd just give her that you-poor-goose look then walk away as if she were a pain in the neck.

Still, if this was going to work she had to ask him for his help, didn't she?

Lost in thought, she turned onto the dirt road. Maybe there was a way to get him to cooperate without really telling him what she was doing.

Nope. She couldn't do it. She had to tell him what her plan was. Explain her reasoning and persuade him that he would be doing all the happy single people of

Mule Hollow a favor. That was the only honest way to go about it. That meant she had to go see him.

She stopped at her driveway and stared down the road toward his place.

Sheri squared her shoulders and drove forward. The worst Pace could do was say no. Right?

Chapter Five

Okay, so she was doing it again.

Sheri wasn't exactly certain why she was hiding behind Pace Gentry's tree-limb-lined horse pen spying, ahem, *watching* him work. She was not a Peeping Tom! She was a woman of action. She'd come here to do what she needed to do, but he hadn't heard her drive up and well, there he was working…and she couldn't very well interrupt him. She could just see the fireworks that would ignite. He'd probably get so irritated that she wouldn't be able to ask him anything.

So here she was peeking through the cracks feeling like a loser but mesmerized all the same.

No, not mesmerized. Entertained.

Okay, she was mesmerized.

The guy had a way with a horse. She never knew something like that would captivate her as it did, but it did. The man could be a real winner if he put a little of that sweet, gentle way of his with a horse into his relationships with people. She had to admit, she could handle some of the attention he was giving that horse. What woman couldn't? Maybe she could make him a deal that if he helped her, she'd help him learn how to treat a lady.

She bit her lip and placed both hands on the wooden fence in anticipation when she realized he was about to step into the saddle. It was unbelievable. How could he be ready so soon to hop on the mustang's back? The fact that there was a saddle on the horse had shocked her when she'd arrived. Now he was testing the stirrups in a way that looked, even to Sheri's untrained eye, as if he was about to swing up there and hang on for the ride.

No, now was definitely not a good time to interrupt him. She needed him to be in a halfway decent mood when she asked him to play the part of her boyfriend. Besides, she wanted to see him ride this wild horse. She felt as though she were about to get the prize out of the Cracker Jack box as she waited with bated breath.

All she needed at the moment was a bag of popcorn and she was set for the show.

The horse's eyes widened as Pace kept his left boot on the ground and used the right boot to put pressure on the stirrup. Skittish, the horse jerked its head and backed up a few steps. Pace stayed with her, talking softly to her and doing a little one-legged hop as he steadied himself by holding on to the saddle horn. When she stopped moving he let her calm down by planting both feet back on the ground. At the same time he kept the hand holding the reins on the saddle horn and contin-ued to talk to her.

It was amazing what a little sweet-talking could do. Would Sheri be able to sweet-talk him?

Sheri could tell by the horse's eyes that she remained a bit uncertain about what was going on, but for the wild mustang that she was, even this much cooperation was nothing less than impressive. As Sheri watched, Pace slipped his boot into the stirrup again. Sheri assumed they'd go through the same routine a few times. *Wrong.* In a swift, fluid motion Pace stood up, keeping all his weight on the foot in the stirrup. It was similar to that first day she'd seen him step into the saddle—only this time he didn't throw his left leg over the horse. Instead, he just stood there, right boot in the stirrup, left boot relaxed beside it, resting against the horse's side as he leaned his torso forward slightly over its back.

Inconceivable! The horse didn't bolt; it just stood there for a moment.

Sheri hadn't meant to make a noise. She'd just been so surprised and awed by what she'd seen that the gasp just happened. It just whooshed out and carried like a shot echoing through the calm evening air, startling both the horse and Pace. In no time the horse whipped its head toward the sound, jumped sideways and kicked its back legs straight out and up, sending Pace flying.

Sheri watched, horrified, as Pace flew through the air and hit the dirt with a thud followed by a grunt. As luck would have it, he landed flat on his belly looking straight at her eyeball blinking at him through the peephole.

Her stomach flipped as his eyes darkened and his lips flattened into a thin, straight line. Unable to move, Sheri watched him as he slowly pushed up off the ground, dusted off his chest, and—without ever breaking eye contact—crooked a finger at her.

Ha! As if she was dumb enough to go in there.

Oh, nooo. She took a step back and watched him come toward her. She thought about running into the woods, but he knew where she lived so she scrapped that plan and held her ground, heart pounding, pulse racing.

"What do you think you're doing?" he rasped, his voice low, his eyes sparking with anger.

"I…" she started, but words failed her when her gaze locked with his. She thought she would be frightened. Instead, she couldn't help thinking that Pace was mighty cute when he was angry.

"Trespassing. That's what you're doing."

"No—"

"Sure looks like it to me. I work with horses alone for a reason, so people like *you* don't come along and destroy an entire afternoon's work. Like you just did."

"Look, if you'd just let me explain—"

"What? That you were spying on me? Lady, I knew from the first moment you came meddling around here that you were going to be trouble. I don't know what your problem is, but I'll thank you very much to turn around and get off my property."

What a hothead! They were at a standoff, only inches from each other with their eyes locked, breath mingling. Sheri hadn't been so mad since the day the posse told her they were taking over her life. But the posse didn't look like Pace Gentry. They didn't smell like Pace Gentry and they certainly didn't make her heart act as if it were going to explode…. Whoa, girl! Get a grip.

Pushing aside her attraction to his good looks, Sheri laid her palm against his muscled chest. It was a reflexive action, like a shield to prevent him getting any closer. But then she felt the beat of his heart against her open palm.... Startled, she yanked her hand away and stumbled back, twisting out of his hold. Instantly, her foot hit a dip in the ground and she yelped in pain as her ankle buckled and she began to fall.

Pace caught her around the waist and swung her back to her feet. One minute she was scrambling to get away from him, and the next she was held securely in his embrace.

Sheri wasn't sure where all the air had gone, but it evaporated the instant his arm wrapped around her. Finding herself being held so close, so carefully by Pace, shook Sheri as if she'd just driven her Jeep over the edge of a cliff. She had never felt anything like it.

She didn't *want* to be this attracted to the man, didn't need to be this attracted to him.

Totally flustered, she pushed away from him. He was standing ramrod straight, his expression mirroring hers for an instant before he once more stared at her accusingly.

"I...I wasn't spying on you," she managed to get out, her voice breathless, her brain struggling to form a coherent thought.

"Yes, you were. Why else would you be here?"

"No! I came because I need a boyfriend," she blurted out because she was so shook up. The second the words were out Sheri wanted to kick herself.

Talk about kissing a good plan goodbye.

In the blink of an eye Sheri saw her master plan disappear into thin air.

Pace studied his neighbor with a fair amount of confusion. He hadn't slept well the night before because of her. He knew she was the kind of woman he wanted to steer clear of, but he couldn't help thinking about her. He knew she wasn't the one for him. When he was ready for marriage, he wanted it to be a commitment for the rest of his life with a woman who shared his faith. Not that anyone would know by his short temper sometimes that he had any faith. Still, from everything he knew of Sheri, she didn't fit his requirements. Besides, he was still trying to find out what the Lord wanted him to do with his life.

Even knowing all of this hadn't stopped him from thinking about his sassy neighbor. Looking at her now chafed him more than he could understand, especially thinking about how she'd felt in his arms. The fact that he was noticing how pretty she looked with her warm, golden eyes like fire in the afternoon sunlight wasn't helping him. The woman was trouble. The last thing he needed was Sheri… Wait…what did she just say?

"You need a boyfriend," he repeated, puzzled. "I thought a girl like you could have your pick of the county."

She tucked her hands in her pockets and surprised him when she nodded in agreement. "I probably could, in all honesty. But I need a special boyfriend, and I think you're my man."

"You're wrong."

Her eyes flashed, and her shoulders stiffened. "You

really know how to hurt a girl." She laid a hand over her heart in mock despair.

Pace didn't say anything. Instead, he headed back to work.

"Look," she said, falling into step beside him. "Would you please hear me out?"

"Lady," he said, not breaking step, not trusting himself at the moment. "I'm not interested. Now, if you don't mind I'd like to get back to work."

"You know, I totally understand why you lived in the backwoods all alone," she said, halting behind him. "You have the manners of a goat."

Pace stopped walking and shot her a look of scorn. "You ever thought it might be nosy busybodies like you who drive a man to the woods?"

Her eyes got all squinty and flashed fire again.

"Good riddance is the only comeback I can come up with," she snapped. "You need to go back to the woods and stay."

"Then you won't mind if I get back to work and you go on your way." He could feel the darts of her scorn hitting his back as he walked away from her.

The last thing he heard was an exasperated huff and the sound of her boots retreating across the rock drive.

As he took the reins of Cinder, the name he'd given the mare that had tossed him, he couldn't help chuckling.

Sheri Marsh did have a way about her, a way he'd do well to stay clear of and stop thinking about.

Still, he was curious as to why she'd come in his direction looking for a boyfriend. He was sure it was only a matter of time before he'd find out.

* * *

What had she been thinking? Sheri fumed all the way home. The man irritated her through and through. They'd had only one semidecent conversation to date and that had ended with him riding off into the sunset leaving her with her mouth hanging open.

The man was a buzzard!

Trespassing, her foot. Hadn't the Neanderthal ever heard of being neighborly? Evidently not.

There was no reason whatsoever that he had to be the man for the posse plan. He was right; there were plenty of cowboys around Mule Hollow who would step up for the job. Of course, none of them made her pulse skip as it did when Pace was around. But maybe that was a good thing. She wasn't even going to think about how messed up her head had gotten when he pulled her into his arms. Nope, she wasn't going there.

Boiling with anger she whipped the Jeep into the driveway and slammed on the brakes when she saw Esther Mae's car sitting next to her house. Esther Mae was poking around in the flower beds near the birdbath.

Groaning, Sheri pulled the car into the carport and hopped out. "Esther Mae, what brings you all the way out here?" She tried to force her tone to sound cheerful.

Esther Mae dusted her hands off and smiled. "I brought you some of my iris bulbs. I thinned mine this morning and remembered you said you like them."

"Oh, thank you," Sheri said, spying the bucket filled with bulbs. She hated being wary of Esther Mae and the other ladies, but she wasn't buying this. Normally she really enjoyed visiting with them, but with them stuck on fixing her "broken" heart she just couldn't let her guard down for a moment. Pace said she was nosy. He should just wait. It was only a matter of time before the posse zeroed in on him. Then he'd head for the hills. Good riddance.

"I think this would be a great place for them," Esther Mae was saying.

"Sure," Sheri agreed, still on her guard, waiting to hear the real reason Esther Mae had driven all the way out to see her. She could have left the iris bulbs at the salon on Monday.

"Honey, are you okay?" Esther Mae said, startling Sheri by laying a hand across her forehead. "You look a tad flushed. Why, your cheeks look like the cherry cobbler I just took out of the oven. Are you feeling all right?"

"Yes. I'm fine. I'll cool off in a few moments." But Pace waltzed across her memory, and she felt her temperature rising.

"I'm singing in the church service tomorrow," Esther Mae said, clapping her palms together, eyes bright.

"You are?"

"Yes. Now I know you haven't been coming to church lately, so I just wanted to come by and invite you to come give me your moral support."

Sheri had not been born yesterday. "Well, I don't know—"

"Sheri, I don't want to hear excuses. We have missed you at church on Sunday mornings. It is just not right looking out there from the choir loft and not seeing you sitting there."

"I—"

"No. I will not take excuses. I am singing tomorrow, and I will take it as a direct insult if you do not show up to hear me. I am your friend, right?"

"Yes, but—"

"No buts. Friends support friends."

Sheri groaned. How did she get out of this one? They were not fighting fair at all. "Okay," she said. "I'll come."

What a pushover she was.

Sheri arrived at church the next day feeling unsettled and preoccupied. She realized that Pace, in all probability, would also be there.

In fact, the second she parked she spotted Pace. The man was just too good-looking, and he was surrounded by the women of the church's greeting committee, including the posse.

She noticed with a wicked bit of satisfaction that he looked dazed and uncomfortable. Had the posse already started in on him?

"You came!" Esther Mae exclaimed the moment Sheri reached the grass lawn.

"I said I would. Besides, really, how could I miss a solo by you?" She smiled. It was hard not to with Esther Mae wearing her grape-laden straw hat. Sheri was actually glad she came when she saw the way Esther Mae was beaming back at her.

"You've met Pace, haven't you?" Esther asked. Not wasting any time to get things started, she swung her head toward Pace causing her hat to slide forward.

Sheri had to remind herself where she was as she forced herself to shoot Pace a smile. "Yes, I've met him," she managed, suddenly blindsided by the memory of being caught in his arms the day before.

"Well, we've known Pace since he was a ten-year-old buckaroo," Norma Sue said, slapping him soundly on the back.

Sheri coughed, covering a chuckle. "I see," she said, biting the inside of her lip. "Has he always been so talkative?" *Or so rude?*

"Always," Adela said, patting his arm affectionately. "I have to go. The piano is calling my name right now, but, Pace, I'm going to be listening for your beautiful tenor voice! So sing out."

"Yes, ma'am," he said quietly.

Sheri blinked in surprise as his tanned neck deepened to a charming rose color around the top of his collar.

The man was blushing. Who'd a thunk it? This just got better and better. Sheri wrapped a finger around a stray wisp of hair and watched him with complete, unabashed interest. Almost as if he realized what she was seeing, his gaze met hers, then slid quickly back to Adela. The older woman patted his arm once more, then walked toward the church. Pace followed Adela with his gaze. Sheri knew he was choosing to ignore her. There was just something about making a man squirm that was fun, especially since he was such a grouch.

"Hey, Sheri," Norma Sue said, yanking on the waistline of her horizontally striped dress, making the lines slope to one side. "I was just inviting Pace out to the house for the Bible study and homemade ice cream tomorrow evening. You're still planning on coming out, aren't you?"

Sheri started to remind Norma Sue that she'd only agreed to think about going to the Bible study, but Norma Sue kept right on talking.

"I invited Simon, too," she finished, smiling smugly.

"Norma," Esther Mae gasped. "Why'd you do that? Did you tell Putts you were inviting Sheri? If that poor man knows she's coming, he'll probably stay home out of sheer terror. If you don't believe it, then watch him this morning. He'll sit clean across the sanctuary from Sheri. And *still* turn white if she glances his way."

Here we go again! Sheri thought in horror. She couldn't help catching the twitch at the corner of Pace's lips.

"Norrrma!" she hissed. "I told you to leave me and Simon Putts alone." She hoped no one passing by could hear this conversation. The last thing she wanted was for rumors to get started about her and Simon. She wasn't happy about the whole situation. The poor man had the personality of a doorstop, and there was no sense in letting any of the other cowboys in on this pathetic matchmaking idea. They'd kid him to death if they knew what the posse was up to. Obviously, Norma Sue and Esther Mae couldn't see that Sheri and Simon were about as compatible as milk and vinegar.

"Y'all don't have a conniption," Norma Sue said. "The man is not a baby. But, Sheri, the poor milquetoast needs a strong woman such as yourself to give him some kick."

She'd like to kick something! Instead she slammed her mouth shut, sucking air through her nose so she wouldn't hyperventilate.

"No," she managed. "I have plans already tomorrow evening."

"What plans?" Norma Sue asked.

Sheri was not fooled. Norma Sue was completely aware of what she was doing. If they only knew what kind of plans she had. Plans that were obviously never going to see the light of day at the rate she was going. Talk about being a wimp—the chant "wimpy, wimpy, wimpy" was ricocheting inside her head. "I'm defrosting my freezer, if you must know."

Oh, that was a good one. Wimp.

Humiliated, Sheri spun and marched away. She caught the glint in Pace's eyes as she turned, adding to her embarrassment. Why, the man was practically hysterical, he was laughing at her so hard. *Ohhhh!* Of all the ridiculous things to have happen this morning. This was not what she'd expected.

Church was filled to the brim as she bumped her way down the aisle. She waved vaguely to friends Lilly and Cort Wells who were sitting in the back with their baby, Joshua, ready for escape if Joshua got rowdy. She made it halfway down the aisle, then decided to go back and sit beside Lilly. That is, until she turned and saw that Pace had slipped into their pew, blocking her way. She'd have to either scoot past him or go around to Lilly's end of the pew, and with the way she was fuming she didn't think sitting anywhere near him was a good idea. She turned away and ran smack into the one-and-only Simon Putts.

So much for the Lord doing her any favors for having come to church. Not that she'd expected Him to do her any favors. His ignoring her was about par for the course, she thought angrily as she looked into the alarmed eyes of Simon Putts.

Of all people—the nervous cowboy almost shriveled up and died right there in the center of the church sanctuary. Sheri was relieved that Adela started playing the piano, signaling that it was time to take a seat. Simon was trembling like a leaf and just stood there blinking at her. He was positively terrified of her. What in the world had Norma Sue and Esther Mae said to this man?

"Simon, relax," she urged. How could they think she was a match for this dude? He was like gelatin. Wiggly gelatin.

"Relax?" he hissed, leaning toward her. "Look, Sheri Marsh, I know there is no way in this world that you and me would ever be a couple. I tried and tried to tell Esther Mae and Norma Sue that very thing. But they won't listen! Said I just needed to give it a chance. Do you know what the fellas will do if they get a whiff of this? I'm the one they'll be laughing at, so don't tell me to relax."

Sheri wondered if he realized that all the hissing he was doing in her ear was drawing everyone's attention. She placed her hand on his arm to calm him, almost choking on the heavy aftershave radiating from him.

"Simon, you don't have to try and date me just because Esther Mae and Norma Sue said you should. Really. Stand down, cowboy."

Determination cemented her decision, and she zeroed in on Pace. There was no time like the present to get things rolling after all. Milquetoast or Neanderthal? She'd take Neanderthal any ole day.

At least she wouldn't be bored.

Chapter Six

The first thing Sheri noticed as she slunk into the pew beside Pace, bumping into him in her haste, was that he was not a gelatin man. No way, shape, or lack of form.

"I decided it wouldn't be right for me to let you sit all alone on your first visit to our church." She caught Lilly's smile from the end of the pew and lifted her hand in greeting.

"Well isn't that neighborly of you?" he drawled, drawing her attention to his impassive expression. "What did you do to that poor cowboy?"

The choir leader asked them to stand and sing. Sheri looked at Pace as they stood up and she raised an eyebrow. "I set him free, if you must know. Now I'm looking for my next victim. Are you up for it, cowboy?"

"Hardly. Too much drama surrounds you," he drawled, then locked his gaze on the front of the church.

That was it. All he said. After that, the man completely ignored her again. To Sheri's dismay the preacher certainly didn't.

Halfway through the service, Sheri felt that Pastor Allen had been reading her mind before he started the sermon. He chose to preach on attitudes. Bad attitudes. As if she needed to hear a sermon on the subject. Due to the fact that her attitude of late had been solely proportionate to what was being doled out to her, she'd have to conclude that she was maintaining a pretty decent one.

Especially now. Evidently, she had inadvertently taken Applegate Thornton's seat. Not that the pew seats were labeled or anything, but everyone knew that the first spot on the last pew of the left side of the church was Applegate's spot. It was where he parked himself immediately after handing out the bulletins. And did he care that she'd taken his seat?

You betcha. Did he sit somewhere else? No way! Instead, she now found herself sandwiched between Pace and Applegate, with Applegate's shoulder and elbow digging into her arm on one side and the feel of Pace's powerful arm muscles on the other. It was downright distracting, but clearly not to Pace. He acted as if she wasn't even there through the entire service.

Why, as far as she could tell by her covert glances, the man never took his eyes off the pastor. There was a moment when she wanted to pinch him just to see if maybe he'd gone to sleep with his eyes open.

But she didn't. She just sat quietly ensconced between Pace's bicep and Applegate's chicken wing and took everything Pastor Allen threw at her. By the time she stood up, the Lord had hammered her toes to the ground. Forget stepping on them—oh no, He'd shown no mercy. That was her relationship with Him in a nutshell. Sheri couldn't get out of the church fast enough. Since she had felt as if God had been ignoring her for so long, suddenly feeling that she'd been scolded didn't sit well at all. She didn't need this.

It wouldn't hurt so much if the Lord got more involved in her everyday situation. She'd accepted for some time that God didn't seem to speak to her on the same level as He did others. Lacy, for instance. After the thing with J.P., well, it hurt that He didn't seem to care at all. It just seemed that if God loved her as He said he did then he'd have been there for her at some point.

But He hadn't been. He hadn't made any effort that she could see. So why should she?

She wasn't thinking about Pace or the posse by the time the pastor closed in prayer. All she could think about was how cold her heart felt. She wanted out. She wouldn't beg anyone for attention…and that included God.

Pace pulled into the driveway of Sheri's house feeling like a royal jerk. From the moment he'd first met his neighbor he'd been nothing but ill-tempered.

He didn't have to agree with what she did, how she lived or the odd ideas she seemed to have. But he did have to stop judging her, and he needed to get his attitude under control. He'd come to Mule Hollow reaching for a new life. He was striving to stretch beyond his limitations to find God's purpose for his life but he felt he was failing miserably.

The pastor had preached on attitude. Pace felt as if the Lord was standing over him during the service tapping him on the shoulder saying, "Listen up, son."

Pace had, despite the distraction he'd felt every time Sheri's arm brushed against his. The woman got under his skin as no one ever had. The fact that she was beautiful and funny, in a snappy sort of way, was beside the point. She was not the kind of woman he wanted to be attracted to anymore. But was that her fault? No.

He needed to get past this issue and behave like a Christian man. That meant asking her to forgive his bad behavior, something he wasn't certain he'd ever get accustomed to doing because of his pride. His pride was going to be his downfall if he didn't watch himself. Thankfully, God had patience and infinite grace.

Pace focused his thoughts on Sheri. He couldn't ignore the fact that something had been wrong with her. Something other than the fact that she was mad at him. There was no mistaking that she'd been white-knuckling the pew in front of them during the last prayer. He'd noticed that she stiffened during the service. When they'd stood and bowed their heads he noticed her hands. She was hanging on to that pew as though it were a life raft, and she was being torn from it by a raging torrent. When the prayer ended she'd almost knocked Applegate over getting out of the church.

No. Pace might not understand her; he might not agree with her lifestyle; but he couldn't in good conscience ignore the fact that he'd noticed something was wrong. His faith demanded that he search her out and make an effort to reach out to her. That is, if he even had any cred-

ibility left with her since his behavior had been so repre-
hensible.

By the time he'd made his getaway from the posse
at church who wanted to introduce him to all the single
ladies, almost half an hour had passed.

Now, as he parked his truck, Sheri came out of the
house. She came to an abrupt halt when she saw him
getting out of his truck. She bristled instantly. She'd
changed into a pair of loose-fitting jeans and a T-shirt
that accentuated her slenderness. The look she leveled
on him said in no uncertain terms that she was not happy
to find him in her yard.

He couldn't blame her.

"What are you doing here?"

Yup, she wasn't happy to see him. "Look, I know
we've gotten off on the wrong foot—"

"That's putting it mildly, cowboy."

He didn't say anything for a minute, trying to gauge the
best way to go about this. After all, he wasn't known for
his tact. He was distracted when a slight breeze ruffled her
hair, blowing a strand loose from where she had it tucked
behind her ear. He watched as it landed across her lips, and
she reached up and drew it away. Sheri Marsh had a beau-
tifully shaped mouth. Wide and expressive, the edges
tilting up so that she appeared always on the verge of a
smile. Of course he knew she wasn't because all it took
was his gaze lifting to her frosty eyes to know she was not
happy. He shifted his weight from one boot to the other,
feeling as if he were at a standoff with a stubborn mare.

Impatient, she brushed past him on her way to the
table beneath a huge oak tree. It had flower beds all

around it, and she'd decorated the thing with dangling do-dads that twisted and sparkled in sunlight. She even had chandelier crystals hanging up there. They looked like diamond earrings, reflecting the sunlight. He had to wonder what would possess a woman to decorate a tree like this, but he had to admit they looked sort of pretty.

Still ignoring him, Sheri picked up a small canvas bag from the table and shot him a disdainful glance. "You can leave now. I'm not in the mood for a fight."

"Look, I came to see if you're okay. You seemed upset when you left church." Light from the crystals danced across her skin. Pink and blue prisms spotted her skin and the ground around her feet.

She pinned him with a glare that might easily have started a grass fire. "Why exactly would my state of mind bother you?" she snapped, placing the strap of the canvas bag around her neck and shoulder. Eyes glittering in challenge she walked over and laid her hand on a rung of the ladder that was leaning against the back side of the tree.

"Well, I—" he started, unable to take his eyes off her. What was she doing?

"Look, I admit I butted my nose in where it didn't belong that first day, and I trespassed on your property yesterday. I got you tossed off your horse like a bean bag. As far as I'm concerned, the only person I'd discuss my state of mind with would be a friend. And I'd hardly say that the conversations we've had so far would lead us to say we're friends. So leave."

Pace deserved that. He knew it, so he took it, though he didn't like it. "Look—"

"No, you look," she said vehemently. "So far, my day,

my week, my summer has pretty much bombed. Big-time. Get it? So, we're done. I need to be alone."

The angry declaration startled him so much that he was dazed for a moment. One minute she was on the ground and the next she'd scrambled up the ladder. When she reached the top, she paused for a moment then grasped a limb for stability and stepped carefully out onto the branch above him.

"What are you doing?" He automatically held his arms out to catch her if she slipped.

She ignored him, reached into the bag hanging at her hip and pulled out a crystal. As he watched, she looped her arm more securely around a tree limb then tied the string to the limb and let the crystal dangle down among the branches. Pace kept his mouth shut, afraid to disturb her for fear she might get angrier, lose her balance and fall.

"Look," he said finally. "We don't get along. That's obvious. But I had to come by and apologize for my bad behavior."

She didn't say anything, but at least she'd let him speak his peace. He forced himself to go on, praying she didn't fall as she stepped farther out on the limb. He didn't know why he was so nervous. From the look of the sparkling things dangling from the tree this wasn't her first time up there.

"Look. Is it too much to ask to start over?"

She grew still for a moment, her gaze darting to him then away. She surprised him when she changed direc-tions and clambered back to the ladder. He was relieved when she climbed down to solid ground.

They were standing so close as she moved toward

him that he could smell the scent of apples in her hair. Her eyes were golden, like clear amber as she lifted her chin and met his gaze. "We can start over only if you'll be my boyfriend."

"What is it with you trying to force me to be your boyfriend? We—" he started, then stopped. He almost said they don't know each other. "I don't get it. You don't know me."

"I need someone who's not looking to get married, yet I need someone the posse will believe I might want to marry."

"Do what? The posse?" Pace stared at her blankly. Maybe she fell out of the tree before. Maybe that was what all of this was about. She climbed up there, fell out, hit her head and was now in serious need of a doctor. "You feelin' all right?"

He wasn't. The woman did things to his pulse rate standing this close. He took a step back, needing the space to clear his head. He came here for a reason and things had not gone the way he saw them going.

She stomped to the flower bed and stared down at the painted rabbit lounging in the flowers. It was holding a sign that said Relax and Smell the Flowers! From the set of her shoulders Pace figured that wasn't happening anytime soon. He kept his mouth shut, waiting to see what she said next.

"Look," she said at last. "The last thing I want is them fixing me up with anyone. That's what they're trying to do. That guy, the one you saw me talking to at church, that's their pick. You heard them talking about me. Stop laughing. This is not funny."

Pace couldn't help it. He'd started chuckling. "I thought they were joking."

"Nooo. They are serious, and that's why I need your help. I took one look at you and knew you'd be a man who would understand wanting people to leave you alone."

She had him on that one, despite the fact that he was trying to change that. He did hate people interfering with his personal life.

"Look, I get where you're coming from, but I can't do it."

She studied him, her eyes unblinking. "Just two dates. That's all I need. Believe me, the rest can be left to their own outrageous imaginations. Seriously. Lunch or dinner at the diner and maybe the rodeo on Labor Day."

"Is lying that easy for you?" Pace asked.

"No. It's not like that. Why is it that they can work their hardest to trick a couple of people into falling in love, but if I want to thwart their efforts it's deception? You just don't understand."

"Sheri, I can't speak for them. I can only speak for myself. Do they actually lie in this matchmaking that they do?"

Her brows knit in concentration. "Well, no," she said at last.

"What you're proposing is me pretending to be your boyfriend. That'd be an outright lie on my part."

"So you won't do it?"

Pace felt sorry for her and disappointed and irritated at the same time. He could only shake his head.

"They're going to come after you, too. I'm just trying to get it across to them that not all single people want to get married. They should respect that."

"If someone doesn't want to get married, then they don't get married. It's simple."

"You are sooo naive."

"But honest. Sheri, a person has to have values."

Her amber eyes darkened. "Well, I guess now you know the worst thing about me." She spun and started back up the ladder. Pace watched her and wished there was something more he could say, but he wasn't good with words.

Especially around Sheri. He kept his mouth shut and left her to hang around up in her tree, praying that the Lord would watch out for her.

Monday afternoon the sun was baking everything, including Pace and the mustang he was working. Lifting his arm he swiped the sweat off his brow with the sleeve of his shirt and continued to work the horse.

It was all about guiding Cinder to take the best deal she was offered. Pace worked patiently with the mare, running the rope over her body, wrapping it around the horse from her halter, down around her rump, and tugging gently so that she could choose to turn out and away from the pull. Cinder sought escape exactly the way Pace wanted her to. The horse had a mind, and a natural instinct to escape. Like people, if a horse thought the path it chose was its own idea, then it complied more readily. It made for a calmer, gentler horse when all was said and done. It wasn't always easy. Every horse was different. Temperaments and personalities made every training session a challenge.

Pace's job was to figure out each horse and work with its strengths and its weaknesses. It took concentration on his part, and today he was distracted. The horse could sense it. Try as he might to keep them away, Pace's thoughts kept drifting back to Sheri. He was good at reading animals and pretty good at reading people. Sadly, everything he'd thought about Sheri was true. She was a schemer. If there was one thing Pace couldn't abide, it was a person who lied.

The fact that she would consider disrespecting Norma Sue and Esther Mae blew his mind, but Miss Adela—that was downright unthinkable. Those were the sweetest women he'd ever known, and to think that she thought she needed to teach them a lesson… Well, she'd lost a marble or two. That was for certain.

To be fair, Clint had told him about the ad campaign the three ladies had come up with to get women to move to Mule Hollow to find husbands. It was like an old-time mail-order bride scenario. Actually, he thought it was pretty smart. It was all on the up-and-up. It just didn't make sense to him that Sheri would think the ladies were scheming to fix her up behind her back. Especially since there were plenty of other men and women who wanted to get married, and it was obvious Sheri was not the marrying kind.

Why should the ladies waste their time trying to change her? Of course, he knew she could change if she wanted to. He had. She had to want it, and it was more than obvious she wasn't interested in that.

The mare suddenly jerked her head, pulling Pace back to his work. He pushed the thoughts of Sheri away and focused on the horse.

The best thing he could do was stay as far away from his neighbor as possible. She represented a portion of his past he was leaving behind. There was no way in the world he was going to blow this chance to prove to the Lord that he was a changed man. Because he was, and once he adjusted to his new life everything would be fine.

Chapter Seven

"Come on, baby," Sheri said, holding the key tight, listening to the engine struggle to catch hold. She was on her way to Norma Sue's. She'd had the whole day off to think about her situation. Despite her plan going south, she wasn't ready to give up on it. No, she liked a challenge. If there was one thing being friends with Lacy had taught her, it was to never give up.

Lacy had called and encouraged her to come to Norma Sue's, insisted that the Bible study would be good for her, and reminded her that there would be homemade ice cream.

Everyone knew sweets were her weakness. Thanks to a fast metabolism, she remained fit despite her love of junk food. Growing up awkward and shy, she'd learned by watching Lacy that an outgoing personality was the calling card that drew people. Not necessarily looks, good or bad.

She learned fast. She pushed that quiet introverted

kid into the deepest recesses of her soul and plastered on a layer of confidence she didn't always feel. It worked. As soon as she'd become the wisecracking, take-me-or-leave-me personality, her life had changed.

Still, she sometimes felt as though she were living a lie. She forced the old doubts away and focused. How in the world had thinking about ice cream sent her chasing rabbits like that? She decided to go to the Bible study, and she was determined to use it to her own advantage.

Okay, she was going if her car would get her there. "Come on, baby, don't mess up on me now," she coaxed, cranking the key again. It sputtered, gave a cough and died right there where her drive met the road. *"Traitor!"* she growled. She hadn't owned a car when she and Lacy first moved to Mule Hollow so when Clint put this old ranch Jeep up for sale, she'd snatched it up. It wasn't anything fancy or new by a long shot, but it had usually carried her up and down her dirt road to town and back without a hitch. That's all she cared about. That, and the fact that Clint let her pay him a very small amount each month so she could afford the payments. Sweet man that he was, he'd offered to give the Jeep to her, and could well afford to do so, but she'd insisted on paying him something.

Being the half owner of a new business in an itty-bitty town wasn't making her bank account any fatter than she was. Not that she cared too much about a robust bank account. If she'd cared about that she wouldn't be in Mule Hollow in the first place. She was here because she'd come to help Lacy achieve her dream. Although, she'd actually fallen in love with the place, despite the part about everyone trying to run her life.

She cranked on the key again and was rewarded with only a dull click. Resting her head on the steering wheel she groaned. Here she'd gone through all of this pep talk for nothing.

At the growl of a diesel engine rounding the corner, her head whipped up and her attitude brightened. Pace was on his way to Norma Sue's, too. She thought she'd heard him pass by earlier, but she must have been mistaken. After witnessing her bad mood yesterday, he would probably want nothing to do with her. She waved him down anyway.

The instant he stopped she yanked open the passenger door and jumped inside, ignoring the fact that he didn't look at all pleased to see her.

"Am I glad to see you. I need a lift to Norma Sue's. My Jeep just dropped dead at the driveway."

"Well, isn't that a coincidence?" he drawled, looking at her as if she just slithered from beneath a rock.

Sheri gaped at him. "What does that mean?"

He studied her for a long moment, his gray eyes almost blue. "I was thinking about your scheme to scam Norma Sue and the others."

She gasped. "Are you saying I'm pretending to have car trouble so I can get a lift from you to Norma's?"

"It crossed my mind."

"Well, I'll have you know that I'm not that desperate. If you don't want to help me open the posse's eyes to the disservice they're doing to the happily single people of Mule Hollow, that's your choice. That doesn't mean I'm going to lower myself to pretend to have car trouble for the likes of you. That's just plain lame. Give me more credit than that."

"Believe me, I give you lots of credit."

She scowled at him. "Look, I don't understand why you're so critical of me. I don't know what makes you think you know me so well that you can possibly understand what makes me tick."

He tipped his hat back and met her defiant gaze. Despite her words, it bothered her that he thought so little of her. "Drive, please," she snapped. "Norma Sue will be expecting us."

He blinked, and she braced for him to be rude. So much for the step forward they'd almost taken the day before. They just took five steps back as far as she was concerned.

"So, how's it going with the horse?" she said as they got on the road. She was clueless as to why she was trying to carry on a conversation with the man, but despite his surly mood she couldn't get the picture out of her head of the gentle guy she'd seen inside the horse pen.

"Fine."

"Been thrown any more?"

"Nope."

"Too bad," Sheri volleyed back and was rewarded with a laugh. Her heart almost stopped beating at the sound. She met his eyes—his twinkling eyes. They studied each other for a long moment. Pace's laughter died like the slow rumble of thunder after a storm, but Sheri saw it. She saw the flicker of interest in his eyes before he blinked it away.

"You should do that more often," she said, finding herself wondering what it was that made this man tick.

"What?" he asked, looking back at the road as he shifted the truck's gears.

"Laugh. Or is it just me that you're so guarded around? I can understand since I was awful yesterday."

He tapped his fingers against the steering wheel. An uncomfortable silence settled between them. Sheri studied his profile, waiting on him to say something, knowing his silence was all the confirmation she needed. There was no laughter in him now. He sat staring straight ahead like a chiseled sculpture. His face was all angles and hard plains, no softness at all. She thought about his smile and how it transformed the look of him. She liked the change. Something inside her ached thinking that he didn't approve of her. She lifted her chin.

"Truth is, I'm not looking for what you're looking for," Pace said.

"What is it that I'm looking for?" Sheri saw that his gray eyes had turned solemn.

"You're not looking to settle down with a husband. Obviously, you like your life like it is." He let his gaze slide back to the terrain as they approached the road that led to Norma Sue's house.

Something in his words was unspoken. She saw it in his eyes before he looked away. Sheri's eyebrows met. "Wait, am I missing something here? My wanting freedom says something bad about me?" Sheri's fists clenched and her stomach burned suddenly.

"Look, Sheri, I've been where you are, and it is an empty life."

Sheri stared at him, reading the tone of his voice instead of his words, feeling as if her brain were misfiring information. *"Wait,"* she snapped as he pulled into the drive behind Clint's big black truck. "What exactly are you saying?" she asked slowly.

He leveled serious eyes on her, and if she hadn't been seeing red she might have been touched that he cared.

"It's obvious you like to date, to fool around. I'm not one to judge you. Like I said, I walked in your shoes until a few months ago."

"What gave you that idea?" She gritted the words out as though her jaw had been wired shut.

"Come on, Sheri. I saw the way all the cowboys were eyeing you that day the mustangs were delivered. You were a regular Mae West out there and very comfortable in the limelight."

"And?" she growled, her ears hotter than firecrackers and her temper about to blow.

"Look, Sheri, like I said, I've been there. I know what it's like, and I don't want to go back there. You'd do well to do the same," he finished quietly and then stepped out of the truck.

Sheri stared at the closed door and felt as if she'd just been slapped. How dare he. He thought—he had the audacity to think—she was a loose woman. Just because he had a past, he assumed...*ohhhh*. He didn't know her at all. Fuming, she was surprised when he opened her door and held out his hand to help her down from the seat.

She gave him an icy once-over. "Oh, please," she snapped, hopping down from the high seat and storming off. "The last thing I need is you opening the door for me." She took a few steps away from him, spun back around and planted her finger in his chest. "Stay away from me." She started to walk off, then whipped back around. "You know, you have a lot of nerve to judge me like that. You don't know me. You don't know anything at all about me."

She was so humiliated she didn't know if she could make it through the Bible study. When she reached the door she sucked in a calming breath and tried to settle the shaking of her hands. Closing her eyes she placed her palms against her stomach and fought for control.

When she heard footsteps behind her she rapped harder on the door and willed Norma Sue to answer quickly. She could hear laughter coming through the screen. "Come on," she whispered, willing the stinging in her eyes to go away, and the door to open before Pace caught up to her and saw just how much his words had hurt.

Pace watched Sheri yank open Norma Sue's front door without waiting to be invited inside. The woman was literally fuming she was so mad. Not that he blamed her. He had voiced an opinion that would have been better left unspoken. Though her denial could have been strictly from embarrassment, he couldn't help feeling a load of remorse. He had judged her, and he didn't have that right. Once again he'd said something he shouldn't have. Why couldn't he keep his mouth shut when he was around Sheri?

"Well, don't just stand there, Pace, get in here," Norma Sue called, stepping out onto her front porch. She held the screen door open for him. He paused at the bottom of the steps, wrapped his hand around the railing and took a deep breath. Back in Idaho he would have been sitting on his horse checking fence line or cooking himself a pan of beans on an open fire out in front of his rover's shack. He wouldn't be standing on the porch of a sweet church lady about to force on a happy face and pretend he was having a good time.

He was way out of his element here.

He was beginning to wonder about the validity of his whole idea of moving to Mule Hollow. Oh well, he was here and he was going to have to ride it out. Sweeping his hat off, he grasped the door just above Norma Sue's gray hair. There was no excuse for bad manners. "After you," he said, forcing a smile.

She beamed up at him. "You always did have good manners, son. And isn't that nice of you to bring Sheri?"

If the Lord had wanted to put him in his place, He did it right then and there. What a hypocrite he was. What kind of manners had he shown Sheri?

"Hey, everybody," Norma Sue yelled, entering the house in front of him. "Pace brought Sheri."

Pace paused just inside the door as everyone turned to look at him. Including Sheri. Looking at her he felt lower than dirt, and it occurred to him that it was just one step back and he'd be out the screen door and headed toward his truck. He hadn't signed on for this kind of scrutiny when he'd moved to Mule Hollow. He swallowed hard. Nothing came to mind to say in return to the odd proclamation. So he'd given his neighbor a lift. What was the big deal about that? That the room was extraordinarily silent had him pulling at his collar and wishing he'd worn his neckerchief to hide the color he could feel creeping up his neck.

Her eyes bright, Sheri smiled suddenly, shocking him since she'd been mad enough to spit tacks only seconds before.

"Norma Sue, don't embarrass Pace. It was just a ride. You know me, no way am I passing up a ride with a good-looking cowboy."

That's when he saw it. The glint of challenge in her eyes and the barely discernible edge to her voice. He was going to have to apologize to her, but not here. Not even if it was apparent to him that the smile plastered on her face was purely for show, and she was really madder than a hornet.

Esther Mae broke the silence as she came flying out of the kitchen in a flurry, wiping her hands on her apron and looking as though she'd just won the Publishers Clearing House Sweepstakes. "Did I hear Pace gave you a ride over here?"

"You heard right, Esther Mae," Norma Sue said, and Pace didn't miss the look that passed between the two ladies before they both turned back to him.

Why did he suddenly feel like prime rib?

"Well, don't just stand there," Norma Sue said, grabbing his arm. "Come on in, and let's get this shindig started."

He didn't miss the laughter in Sheri's eyes, either. Suddenly, he got the feeling the joke was on him.

Chapter Eight

There were a good many people standing around the small living room as Norma Sue hustled Pace around, introducing him to everyone. All the while, he was aware of Sheri in his peripheral vision. First, she was talking to Lacy in the corner near the entrance to the kitchen. They were laughing. When Lacy left the room, Sheri went with her and Pace had trouble focusing on the conversation going on around him. He wondered what Sheri was up to. Plus, his conscience was eating a hole in his stomach.

He wasn't certain what was going on with the sudden twinkle in Norma Sue's and Esther Mae's eyes. But at the moment, they weren't his concern. He'd judged Sheri. He kept coming back to the words he'd said, and every time he thought about them he felt more hypocritical.

He had a past, yes, but just because she appeared to be living a life similar to what he'd left behind didn't mean he had any right to assume things about her. He needed some air and time to think and he escaped to the outside as soon as he found the chance. Clint and Norma Sue's husband, Roy Don, were out by the wooden ice cream machines, and he'd never been happier to see the outdoors as he was when he stepped onto the back porch and saw them.

"You look like you've almost had your limit of socializing for one day," Clint said, grinning.

"You're enjoying my discomfort a little too much," Pace said drily.

"Oh, believe me, I am." Clint's smile broadened.

Roy Don spat a string of tobacco juice. "You two always did have a way of enjoyin' each other's misery."

Pace and Clint had spent many days together roaming the ranch when they were barely teens. Both of them motherless, they'd bonded and learned together to work hard and respect the land. They'd also learned to have a good time while getting their jobs done.

"That's what friends are for, isn't it, Roy Don, to be there for the good and the bad times?" Pace replied, catching sight of Sheri coming out the door.

She was smiling, her eyes twinkling as she practically jogged off the deck. Pace forgot what he'd been about to say. Clint said something, and Pace forced his gaze back to his friend, who was now grinning, watching him with speculation in his eyes. Pace scowled but didn't have time to deny anything. Despite everything that had happened, there was no contradicting that Sheri was a beautiful woman. He was certain Clint saw that he'd noticed the fact.

"Hey, boys," she drawled, looking playfully at him.

Pace immediately went on red alert as she breezed over to stand beside him, all smiles. No one but him knew she was mad enough to tar and feather him given half the chance.

"Norma Sue says to bring that ice cream in so we can get the Bible study started."

Roy Don twirled the edge of his mustache and grinned from Sheri to Pace. "Tell her we're on our way, little lady."

"Will do," Sheri drawled slowly, winked at Pace then sashayed off like she was back on the red carpet.

What was that all about? He decided keeping up with Sheri's personalities was a job and a half. Perplexed, he rubbed the back of his neck knowing full well that Roy Don and Clint were staring at him. His thoughts whirring, he watched until Sheri disappeared into the house.

"So *that's* the way it is. You gonna give me and Clint a hand here, Pace, or you gonna stare at that closed door all afternoon like a lovesick pooch?" Roy Don asked. Pace could hear the laughter in the older man's slow Texas drawl.

"Now hold on. You two better not be getting any ideas," he warned sternly.

Roy Don let out a good belly laugh. "Son," he said between guffaws, "it's not me and Clint you need to worry about. Haven't you figured that out yet?"

Pace got an instant playback of the look he'd seen on Norma Sue's and Esther Mae's faces, and he had the sinking feeling that Roy Don was more than right.

Sheri walked to Pace's truck and waited as he finished his conversation with Clint. The night had been full of surprises, and truthfully she felt a little ashamed. This had been a Bible study and an ambush all rolled into one nice neat package. Something about that just didn't sit right.

Not that she'd planned it, but she couldn't have planned it any better, either. Now that she knew what he thought of her she was shamefully feeling a bit vindicated.

Pace giving her a ride had been the catalyst she needed to set her plan in motion, and now he would see that there was no stopping this runaway train once it got started. From here on out, all she'd have to do was add a little fuel to the fire every so often and the posse would do the rest. She had asked him to participate with her in this venture to stop them from trying to run her life when really, his cooperation wasn't needed after all.

She watched Pace stride toward the truck and pushed away any remorse she might be feeling. The man had insulted her, and this was the ultimate payback. True, she liked to date. She liked going out to dinner, going to the movies. She loved picnics. Hiking. She absolutely loved a good kiss. That didn't make her a *player.* She had morals. She had boundaries, and who was he to come in here and immediately think badly of her?

She crossed her arms and looked straight ahead as he climbed into the truck. She could have gotten a ride home from someone else, but watching his reactions was too much fun. Why, it was so perfect she could almost let go of her anger at the guy.

She waited for him to say something as he pulled his seat belt on, but he didn't even glance her way. Instead, he carefully backed the truck out of the drive and headed toward their homes.

Sitting in the darkness she rolled several conversation ideas through her mind, but didn't feel compelled to try and make small talk with him. No need to mess up the mood. He was uncomfortable, probably confused. She watched him catching the speculative glances all evening, and the poor man had no idea what was about to happen to him. Yep, she could see that on some level he suspected what was going on, but he really had no idea what wheels had just rolled into motion.

Good. It would serve him right, Mr. High and Mighty.

Maybe now he would see what she meant when she said a single person had a right to freedom of choice. He was about to get his very own visual lesson, and that might be the best thing for him.

"You're not going to tell me what happened back there, are you?" he said at last.

"Now what fun would there possibly be in me letting you in on that little tidbit?"

A heavy silence ensued.

"If it's worth anything I shouldn't have judged you like that."

She straightened in the seat. "You're right. It's not worth anything." Oh, she was feeling ornery.

To her surprise he drove the rest of the way without saying anything else. How insulting…the man had given her a half-baked apology and then he'd just given up.

Not that she would have accepted his apology—but still, the man could have tried a little harder.

Like a silent lug he maneuvered his big truck around

her Jeep where it was blocking the driveway. As soon as he came to a halt she hopped out and stomped toward the house, more than ready to get away from him.

Not that he cared. He was already backing out the minute her foot hit the dirt. She had never been treated so inconsequentially in all of her life.

Why, it was all she could do not to turn around and glare at him. But no way was she going to give him that satisfaction. She just grumbled her frustrations all the way to her door and slammed it after she'd entered. He was long gone by then, and she didn't have to worry about him seeing how bothered she was by his behavior. It was a no-brainer as to why the man had always lived in the wilderness alone. *He belonged there.*

Sheri woke feeling as surly as she felt when she'd crawled under the covers the night before. Glancing at the clock she felt even more churlish. She didn't have to be at the salon until ten and it was only six. She hadn't gone to sleep until sometime after midnight so waking up this early was not the best morale booster. How had a simple plan to shake things up in Mule Hollow given her the headache she was having? A headache that wore scuffed boots, clinking spurs and a neckerchief she'd like to twist into a noose around his handsome neck.

She tried to put him out of her mind, yanking the covers tighter around her head, but Pace Gentry plagued her. Plagued her!

All right…he interested her. Rude and all, the man would not leave her thoughts. She closed her eyes, then opened them when she heard a sound she didn't recognize. She sat up, plopped her feet on the carpet, and stumbled to the bedroom window facing the front yard.

She rubbed her eyes, trying to focus. There was a pair of booted feet sticking out from beneath her Jeep.

Pace's truck told her precisely who the boots belonged to. Growling, she stomped to the closet, yanked on her clothes, and stormed outside to see why he was piddling with her vehicle.

"Excuse me," she said to his legs. "May I be so bold as to inquire why you're under my vehicle?" She crossed her arms and tapped her bare foot in the dirt, waiting for him to show his face. The face she'd thought about all night long, whether she'd wanted to or not.

"Hand me that wrench, please."

She frowned. Did he not hear her? Looking around, she grabbed the wrench off the fender and slapped it into the hand he extended.

"Ouch," he said, but managed to hang on to the tool.

She bit the inside of her lip. Hurting him hadn't given her the satisfaction she'd hoped for, and she felt a bit ashamed.

May I remind you the man basically called you an easy woman? Right. On that thought she looked around for something bigger to hit him with. Spotting a pretty good-sized tree limb across the road, she stormed toward it.

"It should work now."

His quiet voice halted her steps, and she felt a bit of remorse at her unrepentant hostility. Spinning around she was shocked to see him already standing with his back to her as he pulled the hood closed. He wore a light gray T-shirt that was stretched across his back. There were bits of sand and grass clinging to the material, perfectly highlighting every lean muscle as he secured the hood. She had the sudden urge to reach out and dust him off. Turning to face her, he met her gaze. It wasn't fair that he was so gorgeous. He had that morning stubble thing going on, and she had to swallow the lump that formed in her throat, noticing how the shirt contrasted with the deeper tones of his eyes.

"W-what are you doing here?" she managed, plunking her fists to her hips and ignoring the ker-thunk of her heart.

"Look, Sheri. I was out of line yesterday. It seems I'm saying that to you constantly. I said some things that I shouldn't have said. I insulted you, and I had no right. Like I said before, I've behaved badly from the first moment we met. I've judged you and you're right, I don't know you." He raked a hand through his hair.

Sheri followed every movement but got stuck on his eyes. They weren't hard as steel today but soft like a dove's wing.

"I'm asking for your forgiveness."

Walking to her Jeep, she traced a finger along the hood. He'd made an effort, so that dictated that she had to follow whether she was ready or not. Glancing sideways, she looked up into his eyes again and realized that she was ready. More than ready.

"You fixed my Jeep?" she asked. He nodded, letting his gaze slide over her face. A tremor shivered through her and Sheri stepped away from him, keenly aware of how close they'd been standing.

"Okay, I forgive you. Now, I feel the need for coffee," she said, spinning away, suddenly desperate to put distance between her and the enticing pull of his eyes and that smile and those muscles…. She padded quickly across the lawn. "Do you want a cup or not?" she called, glancing over her shoulder as soon as there was a bit of distance between them. She told herself it all had to do with her plan, but when he quirked an eyebrow and his eyes sparkled in the early-morning light…her mouth went dry and she had to remind herself to focus.

"Coffee," he said. "Sounds good."

Well, she thought, with lengthy sentences such as that the man wasn't going to get himself into trouble, that was for certain. Watching him cross the lawn toward her, she smiled as a sense of anticipation rippled through her.

Mule Hollow Matchmaking Posse, look out, she thought. The game was on. And it most definitely was going to be interesting.

Chapter Nine

Pace followed Sheri into her house with mixed feelings. He wanted to talk to her, to make it up to her, so he'd come to fix her Jeep at daybreak hoping to speak to her before she left for work. He needed to explain some things to her, needed her to understand why he behaved like an imbecile half the time. The fact that he thought he needed to explain was a plus for him. Until he'd become a Christian, he'd never considered that he should have to explain himself to anyone.

He knew differently now. He knew that as a Christian he had a new code of conduct to live by, and he held himself in strict accountability for that conduct. Strangely, everything seemed to get jumbled around when he was around Sheri. He found himself behaving in an erratic manner around her. It was disconcerting for a man who'd always been in control of everything he did. This thing with Sheri was putting him in unknown territory.

"Sit," she said, as soon as they entered the bright

white kitchen. "And be warned, I don't do early mornings well."

He leaned against the door frame, not comfortable sitting while she was standing. He quickly got caught up in watching her as she snatched the glass carafe from the coffeemaker, wheeled around and shoved it beneath the faucet. While she waited for the water to fill it she stretched her back, leaning to the left then to the right before glancing over her shoulder at him, her eyebrows knitted together.

"Well, sit. You make me nervous standing over me."

He pulled out a chair and sat. She was a moody thing. Cute, but moody.

"So," she said, punching the button on the coffeemaker and turning toward him, arms crossed. "While we're on speaking terms, tell me about yourself."

"You say that like it's not going to last long. Do you know something I don't?" He thought for a second that he saw her cringe.

"Um, no, I was just curious."

He studied her. She was hedging. He could see it in her eyes. The question was why? "Why do I get the feeling you're hiding something?"

"Hey, you came over here waving the white flag this morning. Remember? So talk, bucko." That almost made him laugh. She had the funniest way of firing off her sentences. Sarcastic, yet there was something about her, something he'd glimpsed yesterday. He'd seen it for only a moment when she jumped out of his cab, but Sheri Marsh had been hurt by his accusations. It astounded him, shamed him and was part of his reason for coming here. Sheri intrigued him with her almost chameleon-like—he pushed away the thoughts. He didn't want to analyze his neighbor. He'd come to make peace, clear his conscience and then go home and go about his business.

There was no sound in the room other than the ticking of the clock and the gurgle of the coffeemaker. "You want me to talk. About what?" He didn't know what to talk to her about.

"I know you don't like to talk. Tell me about…"

Pace got caught up watching her think. Her eyes were twinkling in a way that had him thinking again how beautiful she was. *Do not go there, Gentry.*

"Coffee," she snapped suddenly. "How did you make it out there in that cabin up in Idaho?"

He crossed his arms and leaned back in the chair, his gaze holding hers. "On an open fire most mornings."

"You didn't have a stove?"

"I had a gas burner, but when you're in the middle of nowhere and the nearest place to get more propane is more than a hundred miles away, on bad roads, you conserve your fuel. Besides, I like the flavor of it on the fire."

"Do you miss it?"

"Coffee on the open flame? Yeah."

"No, silly. Idaho. Living in that shack out in the boonies?"

He nodded ever so slightly, the grip of longing sweeping over him. "Yeah." *More than you know.*

She took the chair across from him, resting her chin on her fist. Her eyes glistened like honey warmed in the sun. Looking into them, Pace suddenly wondered what it would be like to kiss Sheri?

For Pace, her beauty wasn't all about perfection. The most intriguing thing about Sheri Marsh was her attitude. The this-is-me-take-it-or-leave-it attitude…he wasn't so sure he bought into it completely. He wondered about that rough edge. He'd thought about it all night. Something about Sheri Marsh didn't fit.

Still, it wasn't up to him to figure it out, he told himself once more.

"If you loved it so much, then I don't get why you're here. Lacy said you were here under duress."

The realization that she'd been discussing him with Lacy might have irritated him at one time. Now it didn't. "Look, I came over here to tell you that I've behaved wrong. This getting used to being around people is harder than I expected. I'm not excusing my actions. But—"

"Wait! Cut—" Sheri exclaimed, shooting up from the table. "Coffee first. My mind can't quite grasp the immensity of what you're saying without a wake-up call. How do you drink yours?"

"Black."

"My kind of man—" She laughed. "I might have a sweet tooth the size of a mammoth tusk, but coffee is supposed to be black."

Pace chuckled. She swung around instantly, sloshing coffee on the floor.

"Call the doctor! Pace Gentry just laughed."

"It happens. But you keep that hot coffee swinging around, and we're going to have to call the doctor after you slip."

"Don't try and change the subject. You chuckled. Wow."

She traded the carafe for the coffee mugs and carefully stepped around the spilled liquid. "I'll mop it up after I can function better," she said, setting his mug in front of him before taking her seat and holding her cup beneath her nose, inhaling.

Pace forced himself to look at his cup of coffee. He hadn't come over here to let his imagination run wild watching Sheri. He'd come here to explain himself and leave. That hadn't changed.

They sipped their coffee in silence for a few minutes. He figured if it meant that much to her he'd do well to let her drink in silence at least for a few moments.

"Okay, continue. You were saying you were having a hard time adjusting to being around people."

She had been listening. He lifted an eyebrow and studied her over the rim of his cup. "I just thought you should know that, like I tried to explain yesterday. It isn't personal." That was not entirely true. "Not exactly, anyway. The part about you being a loose woman was completely uncalled for. I only know what I've seen, and you look like you have fun—"

She leveled her gaze on him and set her coffee down with a thud. "That made you think I was a loose woman? The fact that I have fun?"

"With cowboys."

"You mean with men. Here we go again. I get exactly what you're saying. I just don't like it. Didn't last night. Don't this morning."

He was saying this all wrong. "Look, I'm trying to explain. The problem isn't with you. It's with me. I might be a Christian now, and I might like my solitude, but I'm not a saint. I have a pretty sordid past when it comes to women. And if I was headed into town after months of being alone…well, I'd think you were fair game. I'm sorry, but that's the way it looked to me."

Her eyes narrowed. He was not saying this right. He said a silent prayer that the Lord would help him not make any more of a mess out of this bungled apology. "Don't go getting all hot under the collar. I said it was my problem, not yours."

"That's supposed to make me feel better? Despite what you think, I do have standards."

"I know that. Don't you see that appearances…"

She sprang to her feet. "I see plenty, cowboy."

Pace ran a hand over his face and wished for his hat, which was sitting on the seat of his truck. If he had his hat he could pull it down low over his eyes and block her accusing glare. This was exactly why he liked solitude. No explaining himself. No figuring out somebody else.

For a moment he wondered if the Lord meant what he said about calling Christians out. Maybe some people, like him, were excluded from such a command. After all, what exactly did he have to offer the world? It wasn't as if he had an understanding of all of this. Pushing back his chair, he stood. It was time to get back to his horses. At least there he knew what he was doing. Being around Sheri made him think he didn't understand anything. Anything at all.

"Look," he said, searching her eyes for a second. She stood rigid, a challenge in her eyes. The woman made him crazy. "You don't have to worry. I'm done here. I've got work to do so I'm out of here. First, though, I need to know exactly what happened at Norma Sue's last night…other than the fact that I made you mad."

She surprised him with a smile. "Oh, that. Well, let's just say that you are about to become very much acquainted with the posse."

"And what does that mean exactly?"

She crossed her arms, her smile flattened but her eyes laughing. "Oh, I couldn't possibly explain it. I might say the wrong thing. Wouldn't want to upset you."

The woman was killing him. There was no talking to her. It was obvious that she wasn't going to let him forget that he'd insulted her again. Being around her made him feel as if he had his boots on backward. Totally confused, Pace strode toward the door. "Thanks for the coffee," was all he felt safe saying as he shut the door and left her.

He had come here to repair the bridge he'd burned and try to figure out what had happened at Norma Sue's…. He'd come up short on both counts.

Chapter Ten

Sheri and Lacy walked into Sam's diner for lunch. They'd both been busy all morning at the salon and Sheri was starving, nothing new about that. Her mind was still boggled by how their business was growing. True, she wasn't getting rich, but she was enjoying it for now.

"Hey, Applegate and Stanley," she called to the old-timers hunched over their usual game of checkers.

"I think their hearing aids must be turned down," Lacy whispered, taking a booth near the kitchen doors. "That, or whatever they're whispering about is of mega-importance."

"Yeah right, like world peace." Everyone knew that the two older men had something going on all the time. They'd recently tried their own hand at matchmaking, and it had gone awry. "Hey, Sam," she called as he ambled over on his skinny little bowed legs. "I'm starving. What's cookin' today?"

"Sam, watch her," Lacy warned. "She's been acting

particularly peculiar today, and you know how hungry she gets when her weirdness comes out." Lacy made a face at Sheri, and Sheri anticipated that she was about to be drilled about what was going on between her and Pace. Sheri's stomach knotted.

"I made enchiladas today, and I made extra just for you, Sheri. Knowin' how you like them. Even on days when yer not so weird."

"That's my man," Sheri sighed, already tasting the delicious enchiladas. Sam believed in spicing things up and dousing them in *queso*.

"He ain't yer man. He's Adela's man," Applegate snapped. So much for their hearing aids being off.

"She was just joking, App," Stanley said.

Sam crossed his arms and stared at them. "You two just sit over there and hush. I told you before Sheri and Lacy walked in that I didn't want to hear another word out of your flappers while my lunch crowd was in here."

Sheri and Lacy's gazes met. Lacy lifted an eyebrow, and Sheri returned the gesture.

"You guys aren't about to feud again, are you?" Sheri asked. They'd just gotten over a feud that had sent the two checker players to Pete's Feed and Seed for a few weeks. It had just about sent poor Pete over the edge. Sheri wasn't so sure all was well between the three longtime friends, but with these guys it was hard to tell when they were being ornery for real or just being their regular cantankerous selves. Thinking of Pace, Sheri decided that some men were just hard to read all the time.

"Tell him he ain't gettin' no younger and neither are

we. If he's ever gonna ask Adela to marry him he needs to do it soon," Applegate rambled, glaring at Sam.

"Yup, we done gave him pert near two months to get his act together and what's he done? Nothin'." Stanley shook his balding head.

Sheri almost smiled. Without comment Sam scowled and stormed to the kitchen.

"You fellas are going to drive Sam crazy," Lacy said. "Really, he and Adela have things under control."

"That's what you think. We're his friends. Thar ain't no reason on earth why that man don't fulfill the one dream he's ever had in life and ask Adela to marry him." Applegate stood and placed his cowboy hat on his head in a signal that he was about to call it a day.

Stanley followed. "Yep, we figure if we drive him crazy we'll drive him into action. We done found out we ain't matchmakers, but we're pretty good checker players."

"That's right," Applegate said as he strode past them toward the door. "The way you win a game of checkers is by driving yer foe into a corner he can't get out of."

Stanley winked at them as he followed Applegate. "Believe me, if thar's one thang App knows, it's about losing at checkers."

"I heard that."

"Yeah, well I don't hear you denying it."

They griped all the way out the door.

"They never stop," Lacy laughed after the door swung shut behind them.

"Nope, but you know they might be right. Poor Sam."

"Don't ya be sayin' poor Sam," Sam snapped as he came blowing out of the kitchen with two plates of steaming food. The smell was enough to send Sheri's taste buds into overdrive. She was glad she and Lacy had come in before the crowd because despite the fact that he'd made extra, Sam's enchiladas wouldn't last long with a herd of hungry cowboys.

"Sam, my man," she sighed as he placed the plate before her. "I love you. How's about you and me tie the knot and put an end to those nosy matchmakers trying to run our lives?"

Sam frowned. "Eat," he snapped, spun and marched back to the kitchen.

Sheri blinked at the swinging door. "Boy, the man has absolutely no sense of humor lately."

"Love…" Lacy crooned.

Lacy loved to sing about love. Sheri rolled her eyes. "Down, girl. I've got to eat."

Lacy sent her a look. "Okay. Are you blessing the food or am I?"

"Go for it, sister." Sheri bowed her head, feeling a bit awkward since she hadn't said a prayer in a while. Then again, what good would it have done anyway? It wasn't as if He was paying her much mind. "I wonder if everyone said a blessing over everything they ate if there wouldn't be any more high cholesterol and high blood pressure?" Despite everything, she still liked to contemplate things.

Lacy paused the forkful of enchilada that was heading toward her lips. "What does that mean?" She took the bite.

Sheri paused her own loaded fork midair. "Well, you know the Bible does say that as a Christian everything we eat is okay with the Lord. You know, how the disciples didn't think they could eat pig and stuff like that. What about cinnamon rolls and fudge? If we bless it, then I just wonder if that levels out the bad stuff?"

Lacy almost choked on her food laughing. "You've been talking to Esther Mae too much," she finally said.

"How'd you guess?"

"That was an Esther Mae kind of observation."

"Yes, but it is valid. Don't you agree?"

"Good try, girlfriend, but this conversation is not going to derail the questions you know I'm *fixin'* to ask you."

"Don't mean I'm *fixin'* to answer you," Sheri shot back.

Lacy laughed. "C'mon, you know you want to tell me all about what's happening between you and that hunky cowboy that showed up at the crack of dawn to fix your Jeep. Yep, I've got to tell you I saw this coming from a mile away."

"Nothing's happening. Well, nothing really."

"Okay, so what does that mean?"

"Well, the man is a hunk—no denying that, even though I tried. But that doesn't change the fact that the man really gets under my skin. Why, do you know that he actually thinks that I am a loose woman? A floozy, basically." She felt her blood pressure rise just talking about it again. It had taken her most of the morning to cool down. "After he fixed my Jeep and I let him have a cup of coffee, the man was lucky I let him walk out of my house this morning, I was tempted to toss the entire pot of coffee on him. *What?*"

Lacy was grinning so wide that her blue eyes were dancing.

"Stop that." Sheri held up her hand. "Stop that thought right now. I have to confess, I'm getting pretty devious, wanting to give out some major payback. There's nothing wrong with me wanting to stay single."

"You are the one who pushed me to follow my heart with Clint. What makes you different? Come on, Sheri. I'm so happy, and I want you to be, too."

"I am happy, Lacy. You were meant to marry Clint Matlock. Everyone could see it the moment the two of you met. Me, I'm not meant—I'm not," she huffed and slapped her hand on the table. "You know how my parents were—how they are. Nothing has changed. It's getting about time for one of them to add another divorce to their list."

"Sheri, that has nothing to do with you."

"Lacy Matlock, you above everyone knows how I am."

"You betcha I do. You are the best, most loyal, most supportive friend a girl could have. Don't you get that, Sheri? I'm not certain what's up with you and the sudden way you are avoiding God, but He created you special. And someday, you're going to take all of your wonderful attributes and make the most fantastic wife in the world for the man you fall madly in love with."

"Yeah right, Lace. You're talking to me, remember? Save the cheerleading for someone else. Plus, I'm not avoiding God."

"No, you remember you're talking to me. You aren't coming to church. You aren't talking about Him. That's avoidance if I ever saw it." Lacy's eyes seemed to look straight into Sheri's soul. "Everything else I said about you is all true, Sheri. You are special."

"Nine divorces, Lacy. *Nine*. With that kind of gene pool and my wandering eyes—"

"You sound like a broken record, Sheri—"

"Lacy, come on. You can't force me to want to get married."

"Well, that's true." Lacy sighed, then smiled. "But I can pray for the right guy to come along and change your mind. 'Cause I'm telling you, God's got someone out there who is perfect for you, and there is a lasting commitment on the horizon for you. I can feel it. You know what happens when I get a good feeling about something, especially when there are sparks flying every time you mention a certain cowboy's name."

The diner door swung open as Lacy was speaking and Norma Sue came barreling inside with Esther Mae and Adela trailing behind her.

"Did I hear something about sparks?" Norma Sue asked as she scooted into the booth seat with Sheri, not waiting for an invitation.

Here we go, Sheri thought. Her plan had just clicked another notch along, but she had to make this look good. They wouldn't believe her if she acted too interested in Pace.

"Sparks," she said. "There are no sparks."

Esther Mae was almost as red as her hair she was so excited. "*Sheri,* we saw you last night at Norma Sue's. Believe us, you can't hide chemistry like that. The way he watched you, all brooding and intense."

Feeling triumphant, Sheri frowned, took a monster bite of enchilada and didn't say another word.

She didn't need to.

The posse had just kicked into high gear, and they were doing fine without any help from her.

Although she did wonder about Pace watching her. That was a tidbit she hadn't seen.

Chapter Eleven

On Friday Pace was loading feed into the back of his truck at Pete's feed store. He was very much aware of the pink, two-story salon sitting directly across the street from him. As he worked he tried not to look in that direction, but he was all too aware that Sheri was over there working. It looked as though the salon was busy.

Not that that was any concern of his, he thought as he continued loading fifty-pound bags of feed from the dolly. He paused to wipe the sweat off his forehead with the back of his sleeve, and saw Norma Sue, Esther Mae and Adela come bustling out of the salon. They made a beeline for Pace as soon as they spotted him, and there was no mistaking the purpose for their visit.

Pace had never been so uncomfortable in all of his life as the ladies began expounding on Sheri Marsh's outstanding attributes. On and on they went, starting with how nice it had been of him to give Sheri a ride to Norma's the night of the Bible study and how nice it had been for him to fix her Jeep. Of course, he didn't mention that she basically hijacked him. Yet, they acted as if he'd done something extraordinary.

That was only the beginning. They kept on going and going. At one point he glanced toward Heavenly Inspirations and saw Sheri standing in the window laughing. *Laughing.* He was seriously beginning to think the ladies of Mule Hollow were one strap short of a full bridle, as his dad would have put it. In the span of ten minutes, Norma Sue and Esther Mae bombarded him with Sheri's good qualities as Miss Adela stood back lending moral support. He actually came away with some pretty interesting facts about his neighbor.

Such as, Sheri was a pretty plucky gal. Of course, he'd already figured that out on numerous occasions. Something he didn't realize was that, according to them, she'd recently had her heart broken. He'd have never guessed that, except that may have shed a bit of light on her odd behavior and her scheming. She told him she wanted to be single. She hadn't told him it stemmed from rejection. He also learned she was from "good stock" and would make a great mother, that she'd keep a good man on his toes, and that she could be sarcastic at times but that was actually a plus "because whoever married her wouldn't get bored easily." Among all the unabashed matchmaking babble, Pace learned something he wouldn't have guessed in a thousand years....

Sheri Marsh had overcome extreme shyness to become the spunky gal she was. Now that intrigued him. He remembered that she'd told him once that she'd been shy but he hadn't figured she meant introverted to the point of isolation. But that was exactly what the ladies told him.

How could a woman like Sheri ever have been that shy?

He was thinking his neighbor was definitely a puzzle when the salon door opened and she came bebopping across the street. He knew the moment she opened her mouth she was going to be outspoken. Shy? He just couldn't see it.

If she had been as inhibited as the ladies had said, where had that Sheri gone?

Sheri crossed the street, trying not to smile.

"Hey, ladies, what are y'all doing to my neighbor?" she asked, startling the posse from behind. They whirled around to face her, not even attempting to hide what they'd been up to. Watching Pace get paid back for his uncalled-for accusations was such fun.

The man deserved every bit of the harassment he was getting. She knew from watching him through the window that he'd just gotten an earful of information about her and how she would make a perfect match for him.

She knew this because she'd seen him unloading feed and she had casually mentioned that fact to the ladies. Just as she'd expected, they took the bait.

So basically she'd set him up. Since he thought so little of her, she really didn't feel any remorse about it.

"We were just telling Pace what a nice girl you are."

"Nice? Me? Ha! You all know I don't have a nice bone in my body."

"That's not true." Esther Mae laughed. "We told him, so he would ask you out. What do you think?"

Sheri rammed her hand on her hip, playing this up to the hilt. "I told you I don't want your help. For the last time, I don't want a husband."

Pace was watching her. She was still totally against them setting her up, but this was her plan. She suddenly felt a tinge of remorse over the deception she was pulling off. She batted it away like a mosquito.

Esther Mae's mouth dropped open. She leaned in close to Sheri's ear and hissed, "Sheri, have you *looked* at this man? Honey, he reminds me of my Hank twenty years ago. You're planning on passing this chance up? Don't be foolish. We almost have him hooked."

Sheri chuckled; she couldn't help it. If Esther Mae thought Hank had ever looked like Pace, then love obviously altered one's perception. Hank was short, squat and jovial. Pace was tall, lean and as handsome as they came—and as immovable as a fence post.

"Look," Sheri said, deciding it was time for her to get out of there and let the posse do their thing. Poor man, she'd tried to warn him. "Y'all chitchat all you want, but I've got to go. Have fun." She shot Pace one last glance and almost laughed at the steam she could pretty much see coming out of his handsome ears. The man hadn't said one word to her.

She winked at him before spinning away and striding to her Jeep. That should just about do it, she thought smugly.

"Sheri," Norma Sue called out. "You planning on coming out tomorrow for the church work day? We've got plenty of scraping and painting to do and some roof repairs."

Sheri mentally bopped herself on the forehead—the church work day! Everyone was coming out for a work day at the church. It would be the perfect place to be seen interacting with Pace. Not a date, but it could certainly serve the same purpose and with no permission needed from him.

"Is Pace going to be there?" she asked, meeting his unreadable gaze, knowing he probably wasn't going to answer.

"Sure he is," Norma Sue said, elbowing him. "Pace, it will be a great way for you to feel like you belong with us here in Mule Hollow. What do you say?"

He didn't hesitate as Sheri thought he would. Instead he gave a quick nod. "I'll be there. What time?"

"Ten o'clock," Esther Mae snapped. "You and Sheri should ride in together since y'all both live so close together. No sense wasting gas."

Perfect! "That's a grand idea, Esther Mae. Pace, I'll pick you up a little before ten. I'll repay you for all you've done for me over the last few days." And then some.

Hopping into her Jeep before he had time to protest, she waved and made her getaway. This was just going to be too easy. The posse was probably thinking they already had her and Pace in the snare.

Yep. Too easy, indeed!

Chapter Twelve

Pace was waiting for her the next morning when she pulled into his driveway. To her surprise he wore his regular cowboy gear minus the spurs and chaps plus tennis shoes. No cowboy boots in sight, yet still he managed to look head to toe like a cowboy at home on the range.

She wasn't lost to the fact that she'd actually been looking forward to seeing him. She tried to pretend that she wasn't excited about spending time with the broad-shouldered, ill-tempered man, but eventually she'd given up. She couldn't help it that she had fun giving Pace a hard time.

"Hey, cowboy, how's the morning treating you?"

He slid into the seat and fixed his charcoal eyes on her. "I'm looking forward to working on the church."

Sheri was shocked by the good humor in his voice. She'd expected him to be mad. Hadn't he caught on to what the posse was doing? "You are?" she said, hearing the surprise in her voice and knowing he heard it, too.

"Sure. I came to Mule Hollow to give something back to the Lord. Lending my time and muscle to keeping God's house in shape seems like a good place to start." He lifted an eyebrow. "You thought I wouldn't want to?"

Sheri looked away, concentrating on steering the Jeep onto the road. Though it was morning, the air was already dry with heat. It whistled through her hair as they sped down the road. "Well, no," she said. "I thought you'd hate being away from your horses is all."

Pace had a hand resting on the top of the windshield and Sheri couldn't help glancing at it. Pace had nice hands, large and tanned with a dusting of hair that was burnished to a golden hue from the exposure to the sun day after day. She felt a tingle race down her spine remembering how those hands had felt when he'd steadied her the day she'd stumbled. Oddly, they'd been so gentle. Like when he worked with his horses. Now he wanted to give time to God.

Was this Neanderthal actually a nice guy underneath?

She pushed away the thought. He did not need to be a man she could truly come to like.

"So you can paint?"

He quirked an eyebrow. "You've never seen a cowboy paint?"

"Well, of course I have." She glanced back toward the road. "It's just that you aren't exactly like the rest of the guys."

"And you aren't exactly like other women."

"Right," Sheri snapped, irrationally irritated by the remark. "We've already established the way you view me. Let's just stay away from that." Why did it irritate her that he thought so little of her? The man had apologized, sort of. Yet she knew deep down he still had a poor opinion of her moral character.

"You're not all bad."

Was that supposed to make her feel better? "Gee, thank you *so* much. Now back to you. What I originally meant before we got sidetracked—" she gave him a pointed look of warning "—was that you just seem like a guy that wears spurs and chaps in your sleep. I mean, out there in the sticks I just didn't figure there was much else to do but check on your cattle and work your horses."

"You think I'm one-dimensional? Who do you think fixes the fences?" He looked at her in disbelief, and she shot it straight back at him.

"*All* cowboys can fix fences." What was it with them and communication?

"Look. I can paint, okay," he said drily, shaking his head, almost glaring at her.

"Well, you don't have to get all testy about it," she laughed as the church came into view. Yes, indeed, the man was fun to irritate. She wondered if he got any joy out of frustrating her, because he could sure do it. She yanked the wheel hard and they whipped into the parking lot. He was forced to hold tight to the roll bar to keep his seat as they bumped over the gravel parking area.

"You need driving lessons," he growled after she'd finally slammed on the brakes.

"Testy, testy," Sheri chided as she climbed out of the car and strode past him to find out where she would be assigned to work. Norma Sue was in charge of distributing the workforce, which translated, as Sheri had suspected it would, into Sheri being partnered with Pace. The look on his face upon learning his plight was comical. The man surely had figured out what was going on. Surely. But when he didn't say anything she didn't offer any explanations. She could tell as he strode off toward the tools and ladders that he was not overly happy at spending the day in her company. She almost felt sorry for him. Almost.

"Good luck, Sheri," Norma Sue said. "He's acting like a caged-up bobcat this morning."

Sheri met Norma Sue's gaze. "What's new about that?" She jogged after Pace.

"What job did you check off the list for us to do?" she asked, catching up with him. Despite his ill temper she was determined to keep her focus on achieving her goal of making the posse think they had possibilities.

"Roof repairs."

Sheri slammed to a halt. "Excuse me? What did you say?"

He paused to grab the tallest ladder she'd ever seen and settled innocent eyes on her. "Something wrong?"

Sheri gulped in air and lifted her chin as she gave a smile she didn't feel. "No. Nothing's wrong. I just thought you said we were on roof repairs."

"That's what I said. You can find something on the ground to do if you've got a problem with that."

Sheri met his steady gaze and shook her head out of pure stubbornness. "Why would I have a problem with that?" She laughed halfheartedly and hoped he didn't notice the sweat popping out across her upper lip.

"You're not afraid of heights, are you?"

"N-no." Her gaze shot to the roof. It was at least twenty feet from the ground and so steep.

"I didn't think so," Pace said. "Not with the way you were climbing around in that tree."

Sheri smiled, but inside she was fainting. There was a difference in climbing out on a few limbs that weren't more than ten feet off the ground versus climbing around on a roof. She glared up at the roof that seemed to go on and on into infinity from where she was standing. Plus, her tree had limbs to hang on to. The roof had nothing but air to grab if she were to slip and roll off the edge.

"You okay? You look kinda green."

She forced her head to nod. She was too afraid to answer for fear her voice would screech, exposing her terror to him.

She sucked it up and put on her game face 'cause the last thing Pace Gentry was going to see was her fear. Oh, no, this girl was getting on that roof. No matter what happened Pace would not see her sweat.

She'd just have to figure this out. She could do it.

"Look, Sheri." He smiled. "I was just teasing you. I'm not comfortable with you getting on the roof. So you can go do something else."

She should have been relieved by that, but she wasn't. She might be scared to get up there, but she didn't really like being told by him to stay on the ground. "No, I—I can do it. I want to do it."

She was crazy, crazy for doing this. But she was going up there, crazy or not.

He shrugged a shoulder, settled the ladder on it and walked away.

Sheri stood frozen to the spot and watched him stride purposefully toward the church, toting the heavy ladder as though it were a feather. Despite her fear, she didn't appreciate him telling her she couldn't do something. Who did he think he was?

Pace stepped onto the roof and scanned the shingles for damage. He'd stopped by the day before to see what Pastor Allen needed fixed. Pace liked to be prepared. If a man came knowing what needed doing he could be organized. When he'd learned the roof needed repairs, he'd volunteered. The pastor had explained that in several places the shingles were lifting during heavy winds and because of it there had been some leaks. Pace figured the painting and scraping were important but that if the roof wasn't strong then everything below would be weak. That being the case, he'd chosen the job on the roof because he trusted himself to do the job right. Plus, he had experience. He'd fixed many a roof on the ranches he'd worked and this was a simple repair done quickly with a caulk gun.

Standing on the steep roof he spied the first buckled shingle and went to investigate. It was midway up the incline and as he bent down to check the loose shingle the sounds of activity down on the ground drifted up to him. It was nice how everyone was working together. Voices and laughter floated up to him, and he paused to listen. He realized there was another reason behind his choosing this job. Repairing the roof was the most isolated job of all. He'd come to join in, yet he'd removed himself from the rest of the action.

A grunt behind him had him looking over his shoulder. Just in time to watch Sheri crawl onto the roof.

"What are you doing?" he barked, alarmed that she'd followed him and that instead of stepping onto the roof like any normal person would, she'd crawled.

"What does it look like I'm doing?" she snapped, hunkered down on her hands and knees looking a bit green around the gills.

"I'm not sure. I told you to stay on the ground. And from the look of it, you need to let me do this. Now, get back down that ladder before you fall."

"Nope. No way," she gritted out. "I can do this."

His alarm grew as Pace watched her crawl forward, head down and eyes shut.

"Whoa, there," he called. She was inching sideways! She looked like a crab. "What are you doing?" he demanded, now openly alarmed as she stalled in her slow crawl. She shook her head but didn't say anything. Just stayed there on all fours as stiff as a board. "Wait a minute. Are you afraid of heights?" he demanded incredulously, immediately moving down the roof toward her. The fool woman was going to break her neck.

"I'm fine."

The words were almost inaudible. "No, you're not."

"Sheri," Esther Mae yelled from down below. "You ain't moving. You sure you can do that? Have you realized how high it is up there?"

At Esther Mae's warning, Pace saw Sheri open her

eyes and glance over her shoulder. "Ohhh, mercy," she gasped, then glued her gaze to a spot between her hands. He reached her just as she swayed.

Chapter Thirteen

"Whoa, there. I've gotcha." Pace grasped Sheri's wrist, his heart in his throat. "Look at me," he demanded, hunkering down beside her on the steep roof.

She shook her head. "Can't."

He wanted to wring her neck and protect her at the same time. What had the woman been thinking? "I'm not going to let anything happen to you," he promised gently. He knew he needed to get her calm before he could help her. Her breathing was shallow, and he was worried she might faint. He decided he'd save the neck wringing for after they got off the roof safely. "You're not going to fall on my watch, Sheri."

"Promise?"

Pace had to smile. He heard the spunk in that one-word sentence even in the state she was in.

"I promise, but you're going to have to trust me. Can you move?"

She shook her head vigorously. Pace had to wonder

what in thunder had possessed the woman to climb up here. Especially if she was afraid of heights? After all, he had seen her climbing that tree.

Sheri focused on the steadiness of Pace's hand securely wrapped around her wrist and the warmth of his breath near her ear as she struggled not to pass out. She would have no credibility with the man after this. Still on her hands and knees she forced her eyes open and met his gaze. What had she been thinking?

"I've got you," he repeated as if to reassure her.

He'd seen the terror in her eyes. She knew it…but there wasn't a thing she could do about it at the moment. At least he wasn't laughing at her. No, his voice was gentle and his eyes were steady. Though she was frozen to the roof, she'd begun to feel calmer at his touch and the security of his voice. She knew instinctively that he wouldn't let anything happen to her. Still, that didn't mean she could move.

"I can't move." How she hated to admit such a weakness. She didn't have a shred of dignity left. This was a fine fix her silly pride had gotten her into.

Pace's eyes crinkled at the edges when she glared up at him, but he didn't smile. "Yes, you can move."

"No," she said, wagging her head from side to side. The movement made her dizzy so she stopped. "I'm pretty certain I can't."

"Sheri, I have your wrist and I know you're stubborn enough that you can force your mind to do what you tell it to do. Turn around and sit here beside me." His tone was gentle, the same tone he had used with the wild mare. It was Dr. Dolittle to the rescue.

"I can't."

"Yes, you can. Stop saying you can't and put your mind to it. You are the most hardheaded woman I've ever met. You can do anything you set your mind to. Now come on."

Sheri met his gaze again. He smiled. "Come on. Show me what you've got."

"A headache," she growled and he chuckled, his grasp tightening around her wrist. Sick to her stomach and terrified, she forced herself to ease around. The instant she was seated she slammed her eyes shut. He scooted close to her, their shoulders touching as he lifted her hand and securely linked his fingers with hers. If she hadn't been so scared it might have felt pretty nice.

"I knew you could do it. Now open your eyes."

She shook her head. "Can't."

"I didn't know you knew that word."

She nodded. "Not proud of it, but for me when it comes to heights it's ahead of 'aardvark' in the dictionary." Her voice squeaked. She hated this. She'd let herself get in over her head, and now he was going to see that she wasn't as strong as everyone thought she was. He was going to see that she was a fraud. "It's ridiculous, isn't it?"

"But it's real to you. That's something that's hard to overcome."

"Is everything okay up there?" Lacy called. Sheri recognized her voice, but there was no way she was looking down to see her friend.

"Everything's fine, Lacy," Pace called calmly.

"You sure? Sheri, are you okay?"

"She's fine, Lacy."

Sheri opened her eyes and looked at him. "Thank you." He nodded. The last thing she needed was the entire town knowing she'd just freaked out.

"We're just taking a moment to enjoy this great view," he reassured Lacy.

Ha! He was enjoying the view. Sheri was looking only at him.

"Can you tell me how you could climb around in that tree but not be able to get up on this roof?"

She gave a weak smile and shrugged. "It's just different. I don't know how to explain it. For one, the tree was only about ten feet off the ground. Plus, I had the other limbs to hold on to. There's a sense of security in those limbs, I guess. But a roof is wide-open space going upward. There's just the edge and nothing to break my fall. I just have a phobia about it. Always have. Yet I've been climbing trees since I was about four. Nearly scared my mother to death the first time she found me up in one. I can't explain it, but I'm scared of those elevators with the glass, too. I have to stand by the door. And airplanes...I tried to fly once. They had to stop the plane and escort me off."

"And you knew all of this before coming up here?"

He was looking at her as though she was nuts, which she deserved. She was nuts to follow him up here for the sake of her childish pride.

"Like I said, you are the most stubborn woman I've ever met. You probably did it because I asked you if you were scared, and you didn't want to admit it."

Reluctantly, she nodded. "I know. It was stupid of

me." It just about killed her to admit it to him. He would probably pick on her about it for the rest of her life. Then she thought about that and realized he wouldn't do such a thing. And why would she think Pace would be around for the rest of her life?

"So now we just have to get you down without everyone noticing how scared you are."

She hated admitting to him that she didn't think she could turn around, back up and put her foot on that ladder. She hated herself for not being able to do it.

"Don't move. I'm just going to let go of your wrist. Okay?"

She nodded, watching him. He smiled. He was so beautiful. The thought made her giggle, and she was not a giggler. It was proof of her nerves. His grip tightened.

"You're not fixin' to go into hysterics on me, are you?"

"No," she managed and tried not to think about what he'd say if she told him that she thought he was beautiful.

When he suddenly stood, turned around and stepped onto the ladder, Sheri had a near-hysteric outburst. Her heart went wild in her chest, and she started breathing shallow and swift again. Then his eyes were back on her and she locked into that gaze like a life preserver.

He held her hand, and now he tugged gently. "Scoot over here. Don't look at anything but me."

She shook her head. "Sheri, I want to pray for you."

Her eyelids flew up. "Pray?"

"Sure. Sheri, the Lord can help you with this. He might take away the fear and He might not, but I know He will help you get down this ladder."

Sheri didn't want to tell him that she couldn't really remember the last time the Lord had actually done anything for her, but he was already closing his eyes and squeezing her hand. It was a way to put off having to climb over that edge for a few more moments. Pace prayed, his voice low and full of confidence. Sheri listened with mixed feelings, not really expecting the Lord to think this was important. When he was done she felt as though her day of reckoning had come as he tugged on her hand again and smiled.

Suddenly feeling a surge of determination, she scooted to the edge, not daring to let her gaze falter from his. She was a chicken and a half, and the man could see straight through her as he grasped her wrist so her fingers were free.

"Grab the ladder, put your foot on the rung and come on. I'm holding you, and I'm holding the roof. You're not going anywhere but down this ladder with me."

She felt like one of his horses. The man could say things like that and she believed him. Sucking in a shaky breath she did as he asked. The instant her foot met the rung she felt calmer. One minute she was on the roof, the next instant she was on the ladder with Pace securely at her back.

She knew she was safe.

"Okay," he said softly. She felt his warm breath against her ear. "Better?"

She nodded, turning her head to look into his eyes. She felt secure, and suddenly she wanted to kiss this cowboy. But she didn't. Something about kissing Pace Gentry scared her. Her emotions were wound tighter than a ball of rubber bands as she seemed to sway toward him against her will.

"Take hold of the ladder," he whispered, his voice bringing her back to the moment like a splash of cold water. What had she been thinking? His expression was unreadable as he wrapped one hand around her waist and the other just above her hand on the ladder. "Now, move downward as I do. I'll shield you like the tree branches."

Sheri knew that he would. She started down the ladder. Her legs felt weak and her hands felt shaky, but suddenly it had nothing to do with her fear of heights and everything to do with the mountain of a man ever so carefully shielding her from harm.

Pace hammered the last loose shingle down then applied the tar to stabilize it. His thoughts kept going back to Sheri. The woman had been terrified, yet because of her stubbornness, she'd followed him up that ladder. She'd made it down the ladder, and though he'd tried to protect her from everyone realizing that something was wrong, he should have known it would be impossible.

He'd figured out that he'd walked into a setup when Norma Sue had put him and Sheri together as working partners, so why had he been surprised that they were watching them like hawks from down below? The posse and a small group of others were hovering at the bottom of the ladder as they reached the ground. Immediately, Sheri had been bombarded with questions. Reluctantly, she admitted that she'd frozen up there on the roof. He could tell it bothered her to admit a weakness to the group, but she covered it up with her flippant humor. Telling them she'd had to find some way to get Pace to put his arms around her.

That had shifted the attention to him, and he'd decided it was time for him to get back to work.

On his way up the ladder he heard her tell them to stop fussing over her. Just like that she was all tough and brassy again as she strode away.

He had to wonder if what he'd seen up on that roof had been real. Had she really been afraid, or had she been manipulating him? The thought wouldn't go away as he worked.

He stayed on the roof all afternoon, not even going down for lunch. His thoughts were tied up with Sheri. If what he'd witnessed was real, and in his heart he felt it had been, then Sheri Marsh was wearing a mask for the world to see. He'd been privy to seeing beneath that tough exterior for the few moments on the edge of the roof. The woman was not all what she made others believe she was. She'd been vulnerable, and there had been something else, something that ran deeper. He'd seen it in her eyes.

Beneath that brash facade there was a scared woman. But what was she scared of? Why did she think she had to put on an act? These were her friends. He had to admit he was drawn to finding out why.

His gaze sought her out, entirely aware of where she sat beneath a tree working in a flower bed. The woman had as much talent with flower beds as she did with hiding her feelings from the world.

There was a mystery about Sheri Marsh. Watching her

pulling weeds, he realized she'd chosen a job that was removed from the crowd, too. A job that isolated her. He couldn't help wondering who the real Sheri Marsh was.

Chapter Fourteen

"Spill the beans, Sheri," Esther Mae said the second she stepped through the door of Heavenly Inspirations on Tuesday morning. Sheri hadn't seen any of them since Saturday at the church work day. She'd pretty much kept to herself most of that day after making an all-out fool of herself in front of Pace and everyone. She was amazed that they hadn't bombarded her with questions the minute she'd gotten off that ladder. Amazingly, the posse had shown some restraint, but she could read them like yesterday's news and she'd known they'd be waiting at the salon for her today.

Esther Mae was holding open the door for her, ushering her inside as she plied her with questions. Lacy was cleaning brushes by the sink; Norma Sue and Adela were sitting in the styling chairs.

"I don't believe I know what you mean?" Sheri said, strolling past her, dropping her purse on her manicure table. She couldn't help thinking how perfectly everything was working out despite her embarrassing blunder. She'd tried not to think too much about how Pace had rescued her and how sweetly he'd done it. But it was almost impossible. Still, she refused to let herself get caught up in wondering about how much different he was from her initial impressions. She had to focus on what was important, and that was getting the posse to leave her be.

Esther Mae harrumphed. "You know who we're talking about."

"Oh yeah, you mean me and Simon Putts?" Sheri teased.

"Who?" Esther Mae snapped, rolling her eyes. "You don't think we were serious about that?"

"Of course you were serious," she said, knowing they had been.

"We're talking about you and Pace," Norma Sue said. "Y'all looked cozy up on that ladder Saturday. I even thought for a minute there you might get a kiss in."

"Did he kiss you after y'all left?" Esther Mae asked, beaming.

Sheri thought about how much she'd wanted to kiss Pace. "Maybe he did, and maybe he didn't. I don't think it would be right to talk about it." She looked nonchalantly at her fingernails.

Lacy coughed. "You never had any problem talking about what a good kisser J.P. was."

"Believe me, Pace can run circles around J.P. Pace makes my heart do the oddest things." *That was certainly the truth.*

Esther Mae's squeal was so high-pitched that it

threatened to break the glass. "This is sooo romantic. Just think of it, girls. The poor man came here to be a witness of the Lord's ability to change a person, and God has blessed him already."

Sheri thought of their conversation the morning he'd mangled his apology to her and she'd been so mad. He was an honorable guy. There were many layers to him, and she was enjoying each new layer revealed to her. With Pace, she was nowhere near the moving-on stage. Of course they hadn't really known each other long and they weren't really dating.

"Sheri, we have some concerns about you dating Pace."

Concerns? Sheri eyed Norma Sue. When had the posse ever had any concerns? "What's wrong?"

She didn't miss the looks that passed around the room. "We don't mean to rain on your parade, but we've started to have some doubts. Pace, well, Pace is special. I don't mean for you to take this wrong, but the boy doesn't need to get hurt right now."

"Get hurt? Y'all girls have wanted nothing more than for me to find someone new, and suddenly you're worried that I'm going to hurt Pace?" Sheri was stunned. This had come out of left field.

Adela lifted a hand. "Now, Sheri, don't get upset. Our concerns have more to do with Pace's delicate situation. Sunday we were watching him at church, and the way he was soaking up everything the pastor was saying we realized we may have been hasty."

Sheri quirked an eyebrow. "His delicate situation?"

"You know," Norma Sue said. "He's a baby."

"A what?" She shot Lacy a puzzled glance. Pace Gentry was not a baby.

Lacy looked surprised, too. "Sheri, this is the first I'm hearing about this. But come to think of it, it is a valid point. Pace is a very new Christian. A baby Christian who has turned his entire world upside down to seek God's will for his life. It did cross my mind the day we watched the mustangs being unloaded that maybe this wasn't a good time for him to meet someone. Then I decided to leave that in God's hands." Lacy glanced at Norma Sue and Adela. "Are y'all disagreeing with that?"

Norma Sue frowned and Adela looked from Sheri to Lacy. "He's on a journey and whether he looks vulnerable or not, he is. We should be helping him grow and find his way in this new life he's pursuing."

Adela smiled sympathetically. "We love you dearly, Sheri, but we just feel this isn't the time. It is simply that at this time in Pace's life, romance may not be the wisest thing."

Esther Mae didn't seem to echo their concerns. Then again, she was the most enthusiastic matchmaker of the group, never seeming to worry too much about how it happened, just that it did.

Sheri's heart was pounding as she looked around the room at the women she thought she knew so well. Hadn't they just been in an uproar to match her up? Weren't they the posse? They matched up anything that didn't move fast enough to get out of their way. Now they were telling her to back off, to leave Pace alone?

Sheri looked at her friends in disbelief. Once again they were trying to direct her life. It wasn't happening. No way.

They thought they could simply snap their fingers, and everyone would do what they wanted them to do. Date this guy. Don't date that guy. Well, that just wasn't happening.

This was not a posse dictatorship!

That's why before she could think her plan through all the way she opened her big fat mouth and rammed her boot straight in.

"Well, girls, what can I say? Y'all are just a tad too late," she said. "See, I'm taking Pace on a little excursion tonight. Sorry to bust your bubbles, but what's done is done."

Pace was walking out of the barn when Sheri came whipping into the yard. The woman drove that Jeep like it only had one speed. Fast.

"Hey, Pace. What do you have going on right now?"

Looking at the way she was smiling at him, it was hard to remember the way she'd looked up on that roof frozen with fear on Saturday.

He took his hat off and slapped it on his thigh, trying not to think about how glad he was to see her smiling again. "The same as usual. I'm about to pull a fresh horse to work."

"Nope. You're coming with me." She played a drum-roll on her steering wheel with her palms.

"I am?"

"Yep. I need to repay you for—well you know, saving me from my stupidity on Saturday."

"You don't have to thank me for that. Especially since I've been waiting for you to get back to normal so I could tan your hide. What were you thinking getting on that roof when you knew you'd freeze up? You could have been hurt."

He'd been planning to go over and have a talk with her tonight. The woman needed someone to put her to rights when her brain went south. He figured the Lord had put him in her path for a reason. Not to mention that he couldn't deny he was curious about finding out more about her.

"I do have to thank you. So hop in. Besides, except for Church on Sunday, I haven't seen your truck pass my place all weekend. All work and no play makes Pace a dull boy."

He had been working hard. He'd hardly been off a horse long enough to sleep. He had a fresh batch of horses coming in at the end of the next week and he needed to make certain he was ready for them. "I have a lot to get done. A man doesn't have to go into town every day."

"That's not going to fly with me. You don't live in the wilderness anymore, Mr. Gentry. You can't just hole up back here and expect no one to notice. Plus, I owe you."

She held up a hand when he started to speak. "Don't say another word. Just hop in."

He was torn between actually wanting to spend time with her and his responsibilities. "I really need to work—"

"I'm not taking no for an answer. Don't make me climb on the church roof again. Believe me, I will."

Sheri Marsh could be extremely irritating and persuasive at the same time. With her gleaming wind-tossed hair and glowing complexion, he felt himself drawn to her—probably like many other cowboys. He gave one last look toward the corral then gave up the fight, strode around to the passenger side and climbed in beside her.

"You know I've been on a horse all day."

She looked over at him and scrunched her nose. "Then it's a good thing the top is off my Jeep."

He chuckled. The ladies had been telling the truth the day they'd ambushed him outside Pete's feed store. A man would never get bored with Sheri around. "So, where are you taking me?"

"It's a surprise!" She glanced at her watch then pressed the gas pedal. "But we have to hurry."

"Well, of course we do." The woman had a lead foot and loved to spin gravel. Pace had never cared much for surprises and his expression must have shown it because when she glanced at him through the sheet of hair blowing around her face she laughed. When they made it to the county road she whipped the Jeep forward, heading away from Mule Hollow.

"What are we doing?" he asked again. He'd assumed they were going to get a bite to eat at the diner. There wasn't much else happening on Tuesday night in Mule Hollow. Who was he kidding? There wasn't much going on any night in Mule Hollow. Not that he was complaining.

"Sit back and relax. Tonight you're getting treated to a Sheri Marsh dating experience. I figure we need to clear up a few facts you have mixed up about me."

"A date?" Pace met her laughing gaze with a mixture of suspicion and interest.

"Oh yeah," she chuckled. "Did I forget to mention that I was taking you on a date?"

Chapter Fifteen

Sheri loved first dates.

They ranked right up there with first kisses. Of course, on the long drive to the drive-in theater she kept having to remind herself that this wasn't really a first date. This was her plan: she had to have a date with Pace so the posse would start connecting them as a couple.

The fact that Pace had actually agreed to come out with her had pleased her very much. Of course there was the fact that he thought this was a real date. While she knew she should feel terrible about that she was having so much fun teasing him and talking to him that she was pushing that detail into the back of her mind. It wasn't really important after all. He wasn't going to get hurt by this. Neither was she. The man had no interest in finding a significant other so what did it matter if they had a few dates?

It wasn't like he was going to fall madly in love with her—that notion was so totally off the wall she almost laughed. Fact was, she couldn't envision Pace married. He was like those mustangs, a free spirit that didn't need to be tamed.

Knowing all of this, she decided to let herself enjoy the date. She hadn't been out in over two months. Not since J.P. had taken her to the dreaded wedding reception and had the nerve to fall in love with someone else. Besides, she really did owe Pace for saving her hide up on that roof. Despite his moodiness and the bad foot they'd started out on, she was finding that she really did enjoy his company. As the miles passed they talked about his dad, how he'd raised him after his mother passed away. She'd been surprised that he'd given her a peek into his past. But it wasn't hard to see that he took after his father. She could also tell as he talked how much he'd enjoyed his life. It was like his eyes lit when he talked about the beauty of the Great Basin. And as he talked of the land she realized she could listen to his voice forever. Though he didn't chatter her ear off, the man who'd seemed so distant had a gift for bringing stories to life. Yes, there was no doubt about it, she loved first dates.

"Okay, close your eyes," she said when they pulled into town.

"Close my eyes?"

The man was sooo predictable. She lifted an eyebrow and repeated her command. "Come on, close your eyes."

"I don't like surprises," he said, but there was a smile in his warning.

"Listen, cowboy, this is my date so do as I say and close your eyes. And *nooo* peeking. It's your turn to trust me. Fair is fair." That garnered her a long-suffering look, but he did as she asked while she tried to concentrate on what she was doing rather than on how cute he looked with his eyes closed. She was learning quickly that Pace Gentry's bark was far worse than his bite. Watching him she almost ran off the road and had to jerk the wheel at the last minute to stay out of the ditch.

"Whoa! Sorry about that," she yelped, meeting his open-eyed glare with an apologetic grimace. "Close them again, I promise I'll get you there in one piece. That was just a blooper."

Pace shut his eyes once more. He complied just in the nick of time, too, as the drive-in movie theater came into view half a second later. Sheri smiled when she saw the marquee. She loved this place.

Not long after she'd moved to Mule Hollow she'd heard about the drive-in from one of her clients, and she'd fallen in love with it. Though it was a three-hour round-trip drive it was time well spent for a girl who enjoyed old movies. With a good date along for the ride there wasn't anything better than kicking back with a bag of popcorn….

This week they were showing a classic Western with Jimmy Stewart and Henry Fonda. It was an all-time favorite of hers, and she had a gut feeling that Pace was going to enjoy himself. She hoped so.

Pulling up to the ticket booth she placed a finger to her lips then held up two fingers of her other hand. Peg, the older woman working the window smiled and passed her the tickets. Taking them Sheri glanced at

Pace to make sure he wasn't cheating. "Keep those eyeballs hidden just a little longer, mister."

"Yes, ma'am," he said, and she couldn't miss the hint of humor. She liked that he'd loosened up with her. If it had taken sacrificing her pride up on that roof, then so be it. She was game.

Getting the okay to move on, Sheri drove along the rutted path lined with cedar trees and hedges. They practically hid the place from view they were so overgrown, probably planted years and years ago when the theater first opened. Once she was inside the drive-in's circular interior, she parked in her favorite spot, center space, three rows back. Looking up at the huge white screen she smiled. This was going to be perfect.

"Okay, you can look now." She cut the engine and faced him.

"Are you sure?" he drawled, cocking his head to the side, his eyes still closed tightly.

Studying his dark lashes against his sun-kissed skin, she enjoyed looking at him a moment more. For a second, she fought the sudden urge to trace her fingers along his jaw. "Yes, I'm sure."

When he opened his eyes pleasure bloomed across his face.

"This is great," he said, meeting her eyes.

"Cool, huh? I love it here. It's one of the oldest in Texas. One of the only originals left. You know there's a revival of drive-ins going on right now and several new ones are being built, but this—" she opened her arms "—this one is authentic. Come on. We have to get hot dogs, popcorn and cotton candy."

"Obviously, you come here often."

"Aren't you the perceptive one?" she tossed over her shoulder as she hopped from the Jeep and headed toward the red-and-white concession stand in the middle of the parking area. When he held back she turned and waved for him to follow. "Come on."

He unfolded his long legs and stepped out of the Jeep. When he reached her she fell into step beside him. As they walked their arms brushed each other and she found she walked a little closer to him as they drew near the flat-roofed concession stand. Sheri couldn't really explain it, but there was just something about being near Pace that made her feel different. It wasn't something she wanted to waste time analyzing, but it was there. Because of it she had a good feeling that this trip to the movies was going to be her all-time favorite.

There was a medium-sized crowd snaking out the doorway of the cramped building, and the scent of popcorn and hot dogs and sugar permeated the area. Sheri was more than happy to step into the line.

"Don't you just *love* the smell of a concession stand?" she asked, inhaling deeply. When Pace didn't say anything she turned to look at him, only then realizing that he looked uncomfortable. Instead of joining her in line he was standing off to the side. "Is there something wrong?" she asked, immediately giving up her spot to join him.

He bent close to her ear. "I smell like a horse. You didn't let me clean up, remember?"

"You don't stink," she said, leaning close and sniffing. "And if I'd told you I was taking you out tonight you wouldn't have come. Now would you?"

He took a deep breath and rubbed his chin and the late-afternoon stubble that accentuated his square jaw. "No," he said at last. "You're right. I wouldn't have come."

Smiling, she looped her arm through his and tugged him through the doorway. "See? I had to do it this way. Besides—" she leaned close again and inhaled "—you smell like leather and horse and sunshine. Nothing wrong with that. Look at all the envious looks I'm getting because I'm on a date with an honest-to-goodness, one hundred percent authentic cowboy." He blinked blankly at her. "In case you haven't noticed, you're a hit."

The line fanned out into two separate rows and they both took a step forward at the same time. She tilted her chin up and found him looking down at her. Right then and there she was thinking about that kiss again, drawn to him as if there was an invisible thread connecting them. Pace was feeling it, too. She could tell these things. What girl couldn't? He hadn't broken eye contact as they moved forward, and his gray eyes had turned almost smoky…. Sheri sighed, swaying toward him.

"Popcorn?"

Sheri blinked as the girl behind the counter asked for their order in a bright tone.

"Or soda?" she said, grinning.

Sheri's imaginary bubble of contentment dissipated, and she came back to earth with a plop.

"Yes," she said, as she rattled off her usual list of junk food. One look at Pace and she knew that hot dogs and popcorn were the last things on her mind. Even though she dearly loved popcorn.

* * *

"I'll pump the gas," Pace said as Sheri swung the Jeep into the convenience store parking lot. It was eleven o'clock and they had over an hour's drive ahead of them. Even though it was late and he started his days before sunup, he wasn't complaining. He hadn't been to a movie in years. He hadn't been to a drive-in since he was about six when he and his dad happened to pass by one on a trip from Texas to Montana.

"I'll grab us something to drink," Sheri said. "Do you want coffee or a soft drink?"

Pace unscrewed the gas cap watching Sheri walk backward across the nearly deserted parking lot while she smiled at him and waited on his answer. "Coffee sounds good."

She beamed. "A man after my own heart. One large coffee coming up."

He watched her twirl around and jog the rest of the way to the store then disappear inside. She'd surprised him again, springing an impromptu date on him. On first sight he'd labeled her a modern woman. The last thing he'd expected was for her to love black-and-white movies and the nostalgia of watching them played on the tall white outdoor screen of an old-time drive-in theater.

More than that he was amazed by how much he'd enjoyed being with her. She was a barrel of laughs, tossing popcorn at him when he didn't laugh, making jokes all through the show when the main characters were about to do something stupid and get themselves into trouble. Her running commentary was more interesting than the movie. She wasn't just putting on an act for him. You couldn't quote entire lines from a movie if you hadn't seen it many times. The woman was full of surprises…nice surprises.

Still, throughout the evening he kept looking for the woman he'd seen up on that roof. He wanted to be mad at her for climbing up there when she'd known she was afraid, yet he actually liked that she'd pushed herself to try. There was something to be said for a person who tried to overcome their fears. There was more to Sheri than met the eye, and he'd realized tonight that he wanted to get a deeper glimpse into who she really was.

The moon was high and the night was warm and balmy. The coyotes were singing a lonesome serenade while the fireflies danced their little hearts out, flitting from tree to tree and seemingly star to star. Sheri and Pace had arrived home after a quiet drive. They'd talked some, asking questions every once in a while. But much of the ride had been in silence. A comfortable silence that she'd enjoyed sharing with him.

Though Sheri forced herself in many ways to be an extrovert, she remained an introvert at heart. With Pace, for the first time in a long time she didn't feel the need to push herself to be gregarious, to entertain. It was nice….

Like a gentleman he'd insisted on following her back to her house after they'd arrived at his place. He'd checked her doors making certain everything was locked up tight so that when she went in for the night she'd be safe. Sheri was touched by his care. She had to admit that Pace made her feel delicate, vulnerable. She wasn't totally certain about that feeling. She'd fought long and hard to become a strong person. She wanted to be invincible...or at least to appear invincible. He'd seen her make a fool of herself and hadn't once ridiculed her about it. Instead, he'd seemed to relax around her because of it. She didn't want to take steps backward, but there was something about Pace Gentry that was so appealing to that part of her wanting to feel delicate and cherished. It was a scary feeling for a woman like Sheri. The thought of letting her guard down even for a moment was hard. Pace had seen her frozen to the roof like a Popsicle, so she relaxed and tried to be herself with him. That was something she never did, not even with her best friend, Lacy.

Looking at him now, she had to wonder about that. They were sitting on the tailgate of his truck watching the stars and listening to the sounds of the night. It was late, but to her surprise he hadn't been in any hurry to leave. Looking at him, her curiosity turned to wondering more about what made him tick. Maybe if she could understand that, she could understand why she was so drawn to him.

"You miss it terribly, don't you? Your life back there."

He didn't respond at first. Instead, he let the question settle in around him, which was the answer to her question, before he finally nodded. "Most people wouldn't understand. But out there, you're stripped down to the bare bones. There's no pretense, no pressure to be anything but who you are."

Sheri thought about that and could immediately relate. "Didn't you get lonely?"

"A man has to be comfortable with himself."

A woman, too, she thought. "But did you get lonely, wish for family?" It was something she found she really wanted to know.

"We made it through the evening without getting into a fight, and here you go getting pushy again." He smiled at her, bumping her shoulder with his, making her pulse jump.

Sheri pushed back, feeling playful. "Don't avoid the question, cowboy. Do you ever plan to have a family?"

"I don't know."

It wasn't exactly what she'd thought he would say. Why had she assumed he'd say he had no plans to marry and have a family? Pace would make a great father, not to mention husband. If he met the right match…. Suddenly she had an insight into what drove the posse to do what they did. She pushed it away faster than the speed of light. A person had a right to choose her own life, without interference from anyone. She quirked an eyebrow at him. "So, you're just going to be an old grouchy bachelor? You're not going to start playing checkers and challenging Applegate and Stanley down at the diner, I hope."

He whooped. "Not hardly! What do those guys do when they aren't playing checkers?"

"Who knows? Lease their land to some rich doctor or lawyer, I think. They're just retired and not too happy about it."

They grinned, then chuckled, then lapsed into silence again. Sheri loved the sound of his laughter. She looked up at him and they studied each other for a long moment, the air still between them.

"What about you?" he asked.

"Me? No." She didn't want to get started on her reasons for not wanting a family. Her mother's words that "people like them weren't the marrying kind" and her family history rose to the surface and tainted the evening. She looked away from him but could feel his eyes on her.

"Tell me about you," she said, anxious to get off the subject of herself.

"Tell you what?"

"Everything. About life as a buckaroo. I'm fascinated by the thought of it." She studied him for a moment.

He nodded, but she knew he hadn't missed her ploy to take the focus off her. She could see it in his eyes.

"You already figured out that I'm not much of a mixer."

She laughed out loud, and he shook his head but smiled.

"I always found comfort in being out under the stars in the quiet country. I never minded going into town, but I never had much patience for people. Groups especially." He looked up and gave a half smile. "I tended to lose my temper and go back home mad. Most of the time before I finished all my business."

"I have to say, I saw that coming." Sheri pictured him that first day she met him unloading his truck. "You can be a bear sometimes."

His smile was sheepish. "Yeah, well so can you."

"Hey, don't go there, buckaroo."

He laughed at that, holding her gaze with that steady intensity that did things to her insides.

"Why do they call men like you buckaroos? I thought a cowboy was a cowboy. Until I saw you."

"Buckaroo means cowboy. It comes from the Spanish word *vaquero*. But, there are differences. Buckaroos work more in Idaho, Oregon, California, and Nevada. The Great Basin area."

She tugged on the tip of his neckerchief. "It doesn't have anything to do with the way you dress?"

He nodded. "That, too. Buckaroos tend to dress more of the old-fashioned way. Some of it is heritage, paying homage to where we came from, and some of it is that this way of dress worked all those years ago and it works for the buckaroo today."

"How so?" Sheri was intrigued.

"Well, if I'm out there alone a hundred miles from the next person, I've got everything I need with me in my gear. A cowboy, on the other hand, isn't that far from town or a bunk. His saddlebags don't need to be full, and his clothes don't need to offer him as much protection. If he wants to wear a polo shirt, he can. To my mind, that's not appropriate. But he doesn't need to think about that shirt protecting him from the elements, like too much sun or the chill of the night. He might not wear a neckerchief because he knows going out that day that he's only goin' to be out there for an hour or two. A buckaroo's generally going to be out there all day. Maybe all night."

"That's why a buckaroo needs to be more of a loner type."

He met her steady scrutiny and nodded. "That goes without saying. Ranches being the size they are and making neighbors scarce, a buckaroo knows he's choosing a solitary lifestyle. Most times he chooses that lifestyle *because* of that fact, not despite it."

"That's why I don't get it," she said at last. He glanced sideways at her. "Obviously, you loved it. You chose it. Why give up what you loved to move here?"

"Because I felt like the Lord called me to give it up."

Sheri stiffened. Lacy had thought the same thing when she'd talked Sheri into moving to Mule Hollow, but Sheri hadn't ever felt called to anything.

"We're called to be ambassadors," Pace continued. "The salt and light to a lost world. Who was I going to witness to out there by myself? Washing my jeans in the river and cooking my beans over the stove? I saw almost no one in the winter and in the summer, just a handful."

"But you loved it."

Pace met her gaze with eyes of certainty. "I love God more. And I felt like I needed to be obedient."

"Are you having a hard time?"

He smiled. "Can't you tell I'm struggling? It's hard getting used to the bit in my mouth."

She smiled up at him. "Always the horseman. You're a good guy, Pace Gentry."

They studied each other for a long moment. Sheri felt they'd taken a major step toward understanding.

"I need to head home," Pace said suddenly. "I have an early day tomorrow, and the rodeo's coming up on Saturday and, well, I've got things to do. I'd better go." He practically bolted off the tailgate, heading toward her back door before she could blink.

Scooting off the tailgate she trailed after him. On the porch he placed a hand on the cedar post and looked down at her, suddenly seeming almost awkward. It was cute, she thought, looking up into his eyes.

"Thanks for a nice evening," he said softly.

Sheri stepped toward him. "You're welcome. I might have to kidnap you again sometime."

He nodded and his gaze drifted to her lips for a second. Sheri lost her breath realizing that he was going to kiss her…and knowing that she'd never wanted anyone to kiss her more. As he leaned toward her she rose on her toes, her heart pounding in her ears as she closed her eyes and waited.

"Sleep well, Sheri." His whisper brushed across her ear and instead of his lips brushing hers, Sheri felt him step away.

Instantly, her eyelids flew open. Pace was moving quickly away, already halfway to his truck.

Before she could find her voice, she was watching his taillights disappear down her driveway.

It was about the worst ending to the best date she'd ever had.

Chapter Sixteen

Pace liked Jake. He was a twenty-year-old with a passion for learning his trade. Jake was in love with Cassie, a cute girl who lived out at the shelter, No Place Like Home. Pace had been surprised to learn that Sheriff Brady and his wife Dottie had turned their home into a shelter. Pace could still remember how big that house had been. As a kid raised in bunkhouses or rover's shacks, Pace still remembered the first time he walked into Brady's home. It smelled of cookies because Brady had a mom who was always cooking and fussing over him and Clint when they were there. For two guys with no moms they'd really appreciated it. Not that they ever talked much about it. There were some things you hide deep down inside because they have the potential to hurt the most if you admit they matter.

He was glad that house had kids in it now. He was especially glad for this girl Cassie. When Pace met her, he could tell she wanted a family more than anything in the world. He could tell by the way Jake worked so hard that he wanted eventually to give Cassie everything she deserved in life.

Standing in the round pen, Pace watched Jake leading the mustang they'd pulled to start working with this morning. The kid was a natural as Pace had been. For Pace, breaking the horses the old way had been a thrill at first. But it hadn't taken him long to know that too many wrecks with a horse weren't conducive to a healthy old age. His dad had been living proof of that. By the age of forty-five he was an old man because of so many spills off the back of a bucking horse. Even the best took spills, and every time you hit the ground you were at risk of breaking yet another bone, crushing vertebrae, messing up your spleen, or dying in a host of different ways.

Add that to the fact that a green broke horse was just plain unreliable and Pace had decided to come up with a new way. He'd been twenty-one when he'd broken his first horse without any bucking involved. Not that there hadn't been times since then that a horse got stubborn and he'd enjoyed a good ride, but for the most part, if he took his time, he and the horse usually came to a mutual understanding.

"I hear you're ridin' in the rodeo?" Jake said, leading the horse past him.

"I can't let you younger guys have all the fun."

Jake grinned. "We were hoping you were. I mean, you know, it's one thing to break a horse for riding, but there's nothing like ridin' one out of the chute."

"I agree with that."

"Plus, you know it's fun showing off for my girl, too."

Pace laughed, watching him swagger as he led the horse in a circle in the pen. "Yeah, but what if you land on your backside in the dirt?"

"That ain't gonna happen." Jake lifted his hat in salute. "Haven't you heard? I'm the best there ever was."

Pace chuckled. "Yeah, in your dreams, maybe." He remembered being Jake's age and thinking he had the world by the tail. It was a funny thing how quickly life passed by.

"Do you know the Lord, Jake?" Pace was surprised by the question. As of yet he'd never ventured out of his comfort zone and asked about someone's faith. It was new, but he and Jake had been building a relationship over the last couple of weeks and it was merely a progression of that friendship for him to wonder about the younger man's future.

"Yes, sir, I do. I didn't used to, though. I mean, I didn't give my life to the Lord until I moved here. I just thought it was all about me."

"I know what you mean."

"Thing is—" Jake stopped in front of him "—me and Cassie, we're a lot alike. We didn't have much of a Christian upbringing so we're looking forward to raising our kids here in Mule Hollow. We figure what we don't know everyone here can fill us in on."

Pace nodded. "This is a nice place for a family. You've got a solid plan."

Pace pushed away from the fence to give the kid space to bond with the horse.

Pace had a mustang waiting for him in the other

round pen. He headed out, listening to Jake talking to the mare as he went. Jake painted a pretty picture, but Pace hadn't ever given much thought to kids. He'd been a cowboy living a life that wasn't real complementary to families. In a way, it was a selfish way of life. Not all cowboys had it as hard as the buckaroo who lived like a nomad, of course. But for a guy like him the love of the lifestyle made the solitude and low wages insignificant. Most people wouldn't understand it, and a buckaroo wasn't asking them to. Most people couldn't understand it even if it was explained to them.

He'd told Sheri two nights ago, he'd changed his life for the Lord, but honestly, he still had a part of him that was holding out. He knew that with his horse skills he could build a future here in Mule Hollow that would accommodate a family. But…he had his moments, moments late at night when he was drawn outside by the call of the coyote and the whisper of the wind. On those nights he had to ask the Lord to forgive him because in his heart of hearts he knew the lonesome plains of the Great Basin were calling to him.

Truth was, if he had a family it would be hard to ever go back. He hated admitting his weakness, but despite how much he loved the Lord he knew he'd left himself a backdoor exit.

His thoughts drifted to Sheri as they'd done often over the last two days since their date, and he couldn't help but wonder why she didn't want a family. He'd had a great time with her, so much so that he kept thinking about turning the tables and kidnapping her for a date. It was a surprising twist after the way they'd started out.

Being with her had taken the edge off the restlessness he'd been feeling. Besides that, he'd given her a bad rap. He'd assumed things about her that he'd seen on the date weren't true.

That was precisely why he kept thinking about her. He couldn't help being curious about her. Pace was good at what he did because he could read a horse. Look into its eyes and watch the way it reacted to things and know what it was thinking. What it needed.

Though he'd never pretended that he could do that with people, truth was he'd never really been interested enough in people to try understanding them. But something about Sheri kept pulling him, drawing him to her. He couldn't explain it, but for the first time he was interested enough to want to know everything there was to know about a person.

He looked at his watch as he entered the round pen and noted that it was about time for her to get home from work and come jogging down the road.

He'd gotten used to seeing her jog past his place. He decided she'd shown him her version of a great date; maybe he'd return the favor.

Sheri stretched then headed down the road for her run. She needed it after the last couple of restless nights and the posse ambushes she'd endured for the last two days. Despite their supposed trepidation about matching Pace up with her, once she'd gone on an actual date with him they couldn't get to her fast enough to see how it went. Why, Esther Mae practically had them married with a houseful of kids.

Sheri's plan was in full swing and she should have been excited about it, but after their date things were not as clear to her as before.

She was jogging around the curve in the road and was surprised to find Pace on his horse, waiting at the gate. Her pulse kicked up as though she'd just jogged a marathon. The instant his gaze met hers, she knew he'd been waiting on her. He smiled and her insides turned to mush.

She stopped a few steps away from him. "Fancy meeting you here."

He leaned down and held out his hand. "Grab hold."

She grinned and looked skeptical. "Why?"

"I figure fair is fair. You kidnapped me. Now it's my turn."

She eyed the big horse. "I don't know how to ride."

"All you have to do is sit behind me and hold on. C'mon, give me your hand."

Sheri figured if he could save her from falling off a roof he could save her from falling five feet off a horse. She reached up and he grasped her hand and took his foot out of the stirrup.

"Put your foot in there and push up." He smiled when she frowned at him. "Just do it, and do not tell me you can't."

She huffed, lifted her foot and stuck it in the opening as she'd seen him do. Then she pushed as he gave a tug, and the next thing she knew she was sitting behind him on the back of the horse. "That was so easy!" she exclaimed.

He chuckled, and she wondered if he was picturing her frozen to the roof. If he was, he was gentleman enough not to say it, but the grin that played at the corners of his mouth gave it away. Sheri flushed at the memory.

"Now hold on."

Sheri had no problem taking orders on that issue. She wrapped her arms around him and decided that this might be the best beginning to a second date that she'd ever had. She just hoped the ending of this one was better than the last.

They rode in silence for a while, traveling the road Sheri knew by heart because she'd jogged down it so often. When they came to a gate, Pace leaned down from the saddle, and unhooked the rope and let the gate swing wide.

"How you doing back there?" he asked, glancing over his shoulder.

She nodded against him. "Couldn't be better, cowboy."

His smile took her breath away. They rode through the pasture, up a hill and down along a stream. Sometimes they talked, but most of the time they didn't. When he led the horse across the stream bed she felt as if she'd gone back in time. "I suddenly feel like I share something with those who passed this way back in the days of the Old West." She knew instinctively that he felt the same way.

He guided the horse along the trail that snaked along the stream. "I like to ride back here. It's pretty untouched."

That was all he said, but Sheri knew he meant it took him back to the Great Basin. She suddenly realized that he wasn't just taking her on a horseback ride; he was sharing something that was important to him. The gesture touched her.

When they topped a ridge the land swept away to a valley and Pace led the horse toward an old windmill that looked about as ancient as the shack he lived in. It occurred to her, since she'd watched her share of Westerns, that if she'd had on a prairie dress this would be a classic scene. She chuckled at the thought.

"What's so funny?" he asked, drawing the horse to a halt so they could look out across the vastness of the ranch.

"I keep seeing us in old movies. I feel like someone is going to shout, 'Cut' at any moment."

"I know what you mean. When I used to be out there on the range, it sometimes felt like I was living a different life. Sometimes I think God put me in the wrong era."

Sheri loosened her grip on his waist, realizing suddenly that she was still holding on to him as if the horse were climbing a steep hill and she was afraid of falling off. "The first time I saw you I thought you looked like you walked straight off the set of a classic Western. You know, where the cowboy would just as soon shoot you as look at you."

He scowled at her from over his shoulder. "That bad?"

She nodded. "Oh yeah."

He shook his head. "Not that it's an excuse, but the last thing I was expecting while I was minding my own business was to get called on the carpet by a woman."

"Watch it, bucko."

He chuckled then nodded toward the windmill. "Would you like to get down and watch the sunset from up here on the bluff?"

Sheri smiled broadly at him. "That would be nice."

She wasn't daft by a long shot and knew a good offer when she heard it.

The sun was just starting to dip as they dismounted, first her, with Pace steadying her with his hand on her forearm, and then him. In the quiet of the evening they sat on a wide plank at the base of the windmill. Surprisingly, it was weathered but sturdy. Sheri watched the ribbons of blinding oranges and yellows stretching across the sky as the sun sank deep into the horizon. It was a magnificent sight, and Sheri was just as enthralled with the feeling of Pace's arm brushing hers as with the beauty in front of her.

"Can I ask you something personal?"

She nodded when he turned serious eyes toward her.

"Why are you so dead set against getting married?"

Not what she'd expected. She raised an eyebrow. "Why? Are you asking?"

He chuckled. "You know what I'm asking."

This wasn't really what she wanted to talk about right now. It was too beautiful a moment to waste talking about her past. He dipped his head and cut his eyes to her. She gave in.

"You've seen my yard, haven't you?"

"Yup. Never seen so many do-dillys and sparkly things in all my life."

"Then there you go."

His thick, dark brows knit together. "I don't follow."

"It's simple. I'm project-oriented, I love projects. Did you see all my different rabbits? I've got about six of them out there. I painted them all, while I was on a rabbit kick. Then I got on a fat frog kick. Right now I'm on the tree-decorating kick. I saw that in a magazine, thought it looked cool and so I started stringing ornaments up there."

"Whoa, mind telling me what all this has to do with why you won't get married?"

"I do the same thing with boyfriends. Don't look at me like that. Going to the movies does not make me a floozy."

Seeing his confusion she told him about her parents' habit of getting divorced. She wasn't sure why she started telling him everything, but she did. She spilled her whole sordid childhood out right there. It could have been a very romantic moment until she opened her mouth, but it was as though once she started talking she couldn't stop. Maybe it was because he listened well, or because she felt safe with him. Whatever the reason Sheri found herself opening up to Pace. She told him about the nine divorces and all the shuffling that she'd gone through as a kid. How she'd never known from one day to the next which parent's home she was going to be at. She'd been hauled between homes and seen more boyfriends and girlfriends come and go than she had sparkles hanging from her trees. Since her parents lived in the same vicinity, whoever had time for her at the moment was where she ended up.

Pace gallantly listened to her story without comment. When she finally stopped the sun had gone down, and she must have killed any romance that might have been in the air because he wasn't speaking. Sheri figured he'd gotten more than he bargained for.

After a minute he let out a long breath. "What a way to grow up. That's really tough, Sheri. I'm so sorry."

She could see his eyes in the twilight and was instantly furious at herself for rattling on. After all, the last thing she wanted from anyone was sympathy. Here she was trying to get away from the whole "poor-poor-pitiful-Sheri party" that the posse had been having, and she'd gone and opened her big mouth.

"You know," she said, grimacing, "could we rewind over all of that and forget I ever said it?"

He scowled. "It's a little hard to forget. Your parents sound like lost people who need the Lord."

That made Sheri laugh. Leave it to straight-shooting Pace to cut to the heart of things. "Well, yeah, I guess they do."

"It's not a laughing matter."

That made Sheri laugh again. "No. It's not. But the way you delivered that line was funny. You're so black-and-white. For you there are good guys and there are bad guys and no place in between."

He nodded. "That's exactly how I am. Especially when it comes to a parent's responsibility to their children."

"I agree with you one hundred percent on that."

"But not on other things. It's not always so simple."

Sheri stared at him and suddenly felt as if she were under a microscope. A mosquito landed on her arm and she slapped at it, glad to have somewhere else to focus her flash of irritation. "Can we head back in? These little bloodthirsty monsters love me." She stood and walked toward the horse. It was now dark, the ground illuminated by the moon. Still, she looked around for snakes. She hadn't taken two steps before Pace reached out and snagged her arm.

"Sheri, I didn't mean to make you mad."

Sheri looked at his hand on her arm then looked at him. "You didn't."

He stepped close and she could see his eyes flash in the moonlight. "You're madder than a hornet."

She yanked her arm but he held on. "Okay, so I'm mad."

"About what?"

Sheri lifted her chin and huffed. "You know perfectly well what." She jerked on her arm again, wanting to get away from him. "You think me wanting to teach the posse a lesson is somehow underhanded or selfish, just like my parents."

He cocked his head to the side. "I didn't say that."

She glowered at him. "Yes, you did." She jerked her arm hard and almost stumbled when it came free from Pace's grasp.

"Would you listen?" he snapped, yanking her back, saving her from a fall and slamming her against his chest in the process.

Pace had gone stock-still and she could feel his heart pounding against her hand that had come to rest over it. When she looked up he looked dazed. As if he, too, had felt the sudden change in the tension between them. As she stared at him, his eyes cleared and his gaze settled on her lips just before he lowered his head to hers.

Chapter Seventeen

Pace Gentry's grip on her arms tightened as his lips met Sheri's. She stood there, stunned by the intensity of his kiss. Her hands immediately moved to clutch his elbows, needing somewhere to hold. Her head was swimming.

Then, as quickly as it had happened, Pace dropped his hands, stepped back and looked at her as if he couldn't believe what had just transpired between them.

"That shouldn't have happened." Pace's expression transformed into a blank canvas in the night light.

Sheri wasn't sure why he'd looked at her the way he had, but it wasn't an expression she was likely to forget anytime soon. He certainly wasn't going to know that he'd rocked her world with that kiss. She'd been kissed, and she liked kisses, but something had happened to her heart with this kiss that wasn't anything she could explain. With the way he was looking at her now she'd be a fool to let him know it had meant anything.

She plastered on her own mask of indifference and

laughed. "It was just a kiss. Don't get all choked up about it." She flipped her hair off her shoulder and headed toward the horse. "How about that ride home?"

Without a word he swung up into the saddle and helped her up. She'd gotten used to the feel of the horse and only had to hold on to him with one arm as they made the journey. He didn't say anything and she let him have it his way. She was confused about his reaction. Obviously they'd had polar opposite experiences.

It was the longest ride she'd ever taken. She'd never been so happy to see the lights of her house in all of her life. After he'd helped her down he didn't even bother to dismount and walk her to her door, which was fine by her. Her confusion had quickly given way to anger.

What was the cowboy's problem?

It took everything she had not to call him to the carpet on it.

She turned to go up the steps when she just couldn't stand it. Swinging around she glared at his back as he began to ride away.

"Wait just a minute there, Pace Gentry."

He pulled the horse to the side so he could stare back at her. The light from the porch light bounced off his dark eyes as he met her gaze.

"What exactly is going on in your head? That was the weirdest thing that ever happened to me."

"Thought you said it was just a kiss."

"Well, what was I supposed to say? You looked at me like I was a leper or something." She plopped her hand on her hip. "Not exactly the reaction I was expecting."

"Look, you're right. It was just a kiss, and I should have never grabbed hold of you like that. That was inexcusable on my part."

That still didn't answer her question. She was as confused as ever, but at least she hadn't wimped out and said nothing. Sheri stepped back into the shadows so he couldn't see the effect he had on her.

"Forget about it," she said, shaken. "Good night, cowboy."

Turning quickly she walked up the steps and inside her house. If there was one thing Sheri had learned when it came to men, it was to leave them guessing. It used to be fun.

But tonight, as she leaned back against the door and listened to the muted clomp of Pace's horse disappearing down her drive, she wasn't having any fun.

She glared at her empty kitchen, hearing the quiet of it loud and clear. "I'm happy with my life. I am!" She flung her voice toward the empty walls. Her words just bounced back.

After tossing and turning most of Thursday night, Sheri carefully avoided Pace all day Friday. Now it was Saturday and Sheri was running late. The rodeo had already started when she walked up to the entrance of the huge new covered arena that Clint Matlock had recently built at the edge of his ranch. It was a wonderful asset to the entire community, big as a football field, give or take a few yards. There were chutes for the horses and pens near the side for the cattle and bleachers for the onlookers. He even had a kitchen built on one side, which Lacy was using as a concession stand. The proceeds would help No Place Like Home.

Sheri paused just inside the entrance. The place was hopping with a good crowd. Many out of towners had driven in, but Sheri realized that the majority of onlookers were Mule Hollow residents. Looking at all the familiar faces gave her sour mood a boost. It was really nice seeing how the town had grown since that first day she and Lacy had arrived.

Still, Sheri was struggling with her emotions. All morning she'd had to pump up her flagging determination to follow through with her plans. One minute she was fired up and ready, the next she was a coward. She was late because she'd actually pulled over onto the side of the road three times on the way to the arena. Three times she'd thought about turning around and going home.

She hadn't seen Pace in two days. She'd skipped her jog the night before. Her original plan had been to get the posse to think she and he were an item by the time the rodeo rolled around. That was exactly what she still planned to do. The ladies were almost hers, hook, line and sinker. They'd dropped by the salon yesterday, wanting an update, and she'd told them about the moonlit horseback ride. She didn't mention anything else. Norma Sue immediately started talking about how she and Roy Don had taken many a romantic ride themselves.

Sheri wasn't sure what to call what had happened between them but calling it romantic just didn't seem to fit. Disaster, now that worked better. But that wasn't something the posse needed to know.

The sound of the crowd bounced off the metal sides of the large arena, and Sheri swallowed, trying to ease the feeling of trepidation wrapped around her neck like a vise. She wasn't sure why she was so nervous. She pushed away the thought of running back to her Jeep and took a step inside. She had a plan and she was going through with it. Why not? It wasn't as though it was going to matter to Pace one way or the other. After all, he was the one who said the kiss of all kisses shouldn't have happened. She felt her irritation rise just thinking about his words.

"Hey, Sheri, you need my hearing aid?"

Sheri looked at Applegate and Stanley, who were staring at her. They were sitting behind a table over by the steps next to the bleachers.

"Oh, hey, guys."

"We called yer name three times. You sick? You look like ya just ate bad fish," Stanley said, which was ironic because that's how Sheri would have described him.

"If yer sick turn around and go on home," Applegate said, his lips drooping. "We don't need no bug loose in here. That's how epidemics start. A person won't stay home when he's sick and before ya know it everybody's sick—"

"Applegate, I'm not sick."

"Ya look sick. Kinda green around the gills."

"I'm not sick. I promise." At least not with anything catching.

"In that case, do you want to buy a raffle ticket?" Stanley held up a silver belt buckle that resembled a hubcap. The overhead light reflected off it and almost blinded Sheri.

"You guys could have gotten a bigger buckle, couldn't you?" she asked wryly.

"See?" Applegate said, glaring at Stanley. "I told ya we needed a bigger one."

"We didn't need it no bigger," Stanley answered.

"She said it was too little—"

"Guys, I was just joking. Really. Believe me that one is plenty big. A family of four could eat lunch on it."

Stanley and Applegate turned matching frowns on her.

"Okay, okay, sorry. The buckle is lovely. Perfect." *For a sled,* she thought. Tugging a few bills from her pocket she handed them to Applegate. He took the money with two fingers and placed it inside the cardboard cigar box as if trying to avoid "the bug" she might be lying about having.

Sheri heard Roy Don's voice crackle over the loud-speakers letting everyone know the bronc riding event was about to start.

"Thanks," she said. Taking her raffle tickets she headed toward the concession stand. She was feeling queasy despite her denials, but it had nothing to do with a bug. Except maybe a pesky mosquito named Pace.

"Hi, Sheri," Lilly said from across the counter when she spotted Sheri approaching. Lacy was behind her in the doorway to the kitchen storeroom looking like the Pillsbury dough girl. Behind her a smokelike plume of flour hovered.

"What happened to you?" Sheri looked from Lacy to Lilly.

Lilly was biting her lip, openly trying not to laugh.

"Hey, no giggling. I could ask the same thing about

you," Lacy volleyed, then coughed. "You're kind of green."

What was it with the green remarks! "And you look like you just had a fight with a hundred-pound sack of flour. And lost."

Lilly finally let the chuckle escape. "It was a ten-pound bag."

Lacy dropped her ghostly white hands to her hips and huffed, stirring up a new plume. "Hey, so I learned that dropping a bag of flour can be a health hazard. It's all good."

Sheri watched Lacy beat flour off herself. "Lilly, do you need my help back there? Lacy could be at that all day." Sheri really wished they'd make her work so she couldn't go through with her plan. "You know I offered before, but Lacy said no."

"It's still no, Sheri," Lacy said firmly. "I already told you that we can't afford for you to work the concession stand. Remember, we are trying to make a profit to help the shelter. If you come back here, all of that—" Lacy waved a hand toward the counter where Sheri had already spotted the mouthwatering array of fudge, candies and cakes waiting to be sold off "—will be gone."

"I wouldn't eat all of it," Sheri grumbled in self-defense. True, she would start with Dottie's peanut butter fudge and then have a cluster or two…and of course there was the to-die-for peanut brittle—

"But you would try." Lacy broke into her thoughts with a knowing look.

"So sue me if I happen to be crazy about Dottie's candies."

"Crazy is right. Just do yourself and us a favor and *buy* an assortment. Then have a seat in the stands and enjoy the show. We know you want to watch Pace ride."

Sheri frowned at that. She should have been happy. Her goal was basically accomplished. She was linked to Pace in everyone's minds. All she needed to do now was make the posse see sparks and within days she'd be done with her charade. Her farce.

"Yep, yep, yep, word's out," Lacy quipped in her signature tone—the one she used when she was really excited about something. "Everyone knows about you two. Esther Mae and Norma Sue have been busy little bees."

"I think it's really nice," Lilly added. Walking over, she set a bag of candy on the counter for Sheri. "It's about time for you to find someone else. J.P. wasn't for you."

Sheri's conscience pricked. These were her friends, and Pace was right. She was deceiving them. "Is that for me?" she said, feeling like a weasel.

"Yes. I put all your favorites in there." Lilly smiled.

Sheri dug a twenty from her pocket and handed it over. "No, keep the change for a donation," she said when Lilly held out three fives. Feeling the need to get away as quickly as possible, Sheri waved and headed toward the stands.

Lacy stopped her before she'd gotten too far. Walking around the counter, a trail of white trailing on the floor with every step she took she asked, "You okay? Really?"

Leave it to Lacy to know her. In the beginning this seemed so easy. Now she felt like a heel.

"Fine. I'm fine," she managed, avoiding her friend's eyes. Lacy was funny, fun and about the most intuitive person Sheri had ever met. Sheri knew it wouldn't take much for Lacy to see through her.

"You know I'm just teasing you," Lacy said. "Remember, I'm rooting for when or if you've met your match."

Met her match…the thought of it made Sheri feel greener than everyone was telling her she looked.

Pace Gentry did something to her. Every time she was around him the man sent her world spinning. That kiss that "shouldn't have happened" had been different. She'd tried not to think about it. Tried to convince herself it had just been a kiss. But it had reached her heart.

She took a bite of fudge to hide any expression that might alert Lacy to the turmoil churning inside her.

"I gotta go." Sheri was suddenly desperate to get to the top of the bleachers away from everyone. With effort she smiled then sidestepped Lacy and took the bleachers two at a time.

She didn't miss Lacy's chuckles behind her.

"Pace, hi. I'm Rita. Remember? Norma Sue introduced us at church."

Pace tore his eyes away from watching Sheri jog to the top of the bleachers and focused on the blond woman smiling at him. He vaguely remembered seeing her before. "I remember," he said, his eyes moving back toward Sheri. He hadn't been able to stop thinking about her since he rode off like a coward after kissing her.

"Are you going to ride?"

What? He looked back at the woman. Rita. "Yeah, broncs. Can I do something for you?"

She smiled, and he realized she was a nice-looking lady, and he could not have cared less. He met Sheri's gaze across the crowd. She didn't look happy. Matter of fact, she had a scowl on her face that would scare a horse thief. Rita was droning on beside him, as Sheri suddenly plastered a smile on her face and wiggled her fingers at him. She'd done the same thing the morning the mustangs arrived, wiggled her fingers at him as if drumming on air rapidly with the tips.

He didn't smile back. He figured his scowl matched the one she'd just thrown off. The woman dug into his moods like a thorn into soft flesh. He hadn't been able to understand what had happened to him that night at the windmill. One minute they'd been getting on great as he got a glimpse of her past. He'd seen another side to her and he'd felt something shift inside him. He tried to fight it, because Sheri seemed to live in a spiritual gray zone. Picking and choosing whatever suited her from what he knew to be right or wrong.

Kissing her had come as a surprise to him. But he hadn't gotten over it yet.

"—around. That would be nice. Pace—"

"What?" he stammered, glancing at Rita as she laid her hand on his arm.

She smiled, squeezing his arm. "I said I was thinking about moving here and wondered if you could show me around?"

Pace glanced down at the slender hand on his arm and then at the deep blue eyes. "I'm sorry, miss. I'm pretty covered up in work right now. Maybe you could ask one of these other guys."

She pouted, tucking her chin in, and Pace contrasted her with Sheri. Sheri wouldn't pout if someone offered her a thousand bucks. He glanced back at Rita's hand that was now tracing a long fingernail along his forearm. He felt nothing. Pace thought of the way he felt just sitting next to Sheri. Their shoulders were barely touching and he'd felt a connection all the way down to the tips of his toes. He wasn't even going to think about what the kiss had done. He'd been feeling as if he'd gotten bucked off a two-bit bronc ever since.

"Please," Rita cooed.

Having had enough, Pace stepped away from Rita's touch. "Excuse me. It's time for my ride. But you have a nice day."

He strode toward the chute, yanking his gloves on as he went, more than glad to climb into the saddle. Matter of fact, he thought as he climbed the steel rungs of the gate and looked down into the chute at the bronc, he hoped he drew the rowdiest ride in the building.

He figured if he had any luck at all he'd get bucked off and kicked in the head. At least then he'd have an excuse for the crazy thoughts that had been flowing through his brain since he'd grabbed hold of Sheri and kissed her.

Thoughts that almost surged up again, but he forced them away by climbing over the gate and easing into the saddle. Pace knew the instant he took the reins that he'd gotten his wish. As he waited to give the nod for the gate to open, there was no mistaking by the fit the horse was throwing that he'd drawn a bronc that was as ready for a fight as he was.

Chapter Eighteen

"This arena is just lovely," Adela said, walking up and taking a seat beside Norma Sue. "Aren't we blessed that Clint has this and has opened it up for our enjoyment?"

"I'm certainly glad for the shade. It's hot enough to fry eggs out there on the concrete," Esther Mae said as she fiddled with her stadium seat.

"That's the truth," Norma Sue agreed, fanning herself with her straw hat. "Look, our boy is in the saddle," she said, glancing at Sheri.

Sheri chomped on a piece of chocolate and tried not to show her foul mood. After all, she was supposed to be happy. As far as they knew, she was falling in love with the curmudgeon who had just lowered himself into the chute with what looked like a maniac horse.

"Look at the storm that bronc is brewing." Norma Sue chuckled. "Whew wee! It's ready for a fight."

Sheri swallowed and felt queasy. The animal did look

mean. But Pace's expression said he was ready for anything the bronc threw at him.

Still she felt a bit of trepidation.

"This is going to be good," Norma Sue said, her voice full of excitement. "Poetry in motion. That's what Pace is when he's on the back of a bronc."

Esther Mae swung around and smiled up at Sheri. "That's right, I can still remember the first time we saw him ride. He was the cutest young boy, and it was on a steer, but I could just tell he was a natural. It's with great alacrity that I came to watch him ride today."

"What in the world did you just say?" Norma Sue asked. "Al-a-what?"

Esther Mae jutted her chin out and lifted her nose in the air. "Alacrity, it means eagerness. It's another one of my new words from the Reader's Digest."

"Esther Mae, you're driving me batty," Norma Sue said. "Here we were talking about Pace and now I've clean forgot what we were sayin'."

Esther Mae dropped her chin to her chest. "Exactly why you need to be practicing this brainpower thing, Norma Sue. It'll help you not forget so easily."

Norma Sue shook her head. "That was just a figure of speech, Esther. Of course I remember what we were talking about."

"Oh, here he goes!" Esther Mae exclaimed.

Sheri's attention had already shifted away from the ladies. She'd watched Pace give the nod and the gate swing open. She and everyone else surged to their feet as the horse exploded into the arena.

It twisted and bucked and kicked in wild erratic contortions, but Pace's body moved with the horse in a beautiful rhythmic flow. He leaned back, almost lying down on the horse's back, his left arm raised above his head. Watching him, Sheri couldn't help but think that everything she'd heard was true. It was as if he anticipated the horse's every movement. When the other cowboys started whistling and cheering she knew that he was spectacular. The man could ride a horse and even his peers were agreeing. It was unforgettable.

When the buzzer sounded he waved his hat to the cheering crowd and sprang from the bronc's back in a graceful movement, landing on his feet as light as a cat.

Sheri's heart slammed into her throat. This was the moment she'd planned out carefully, and she had to do it.

Over the last two days, she had come to the conclusion that Pace Gentry was not going to hold any kind of power over her, and for the last few days that was exactly what she had felt he was doing. She couldn't explain it, but thoughts of him had filled her head every moment. The man made her weak in the knees.

It wasn't good.

It was time to get this over with.

She dropped her bag of candy and before she could lose her nerve she jogged down the bleachers. He was coming out of the gate, working his leather gloves off his hands when she stepped into his path. Sweat gleamed on his forehead, and his eyes were bright from the adrenaline that she was certain still pumped through his veins.

She almost turned and ran, but good, bad or just plain crazy she was finishing what she'd started.

"You can sure ride, cowboy," she managed, ignoring the voice telling her to back off. She slipped her arms around his neck in front of the entire crowd and kissed him.

The instant her lips touched his, Pace wrapped one arm around her, pulled her close and—just as he'd done standing beside the windmill—he turned her world upside down.

That had not been in her plan.

The last thing Pace had expected was for Sheri to come along and throw herself into his arms. He had to admit it was the perfect end to a great ride. Every alarm bell in his head was going off but he wasn't listening. Riding the wave of adrenaline, he gave in to the feel of her lips. This time, it was Sheri who finally pulled away. She backed out of his embrace, her fingers on her lips and her eyes alive.

Pace stood right there in that arena and let the truth settle over him. He had a problem. No matter how much he knew he needed to stay clear of his neighbor, she stirred feelings inside him that he'd never felt before. He'd gotten a hint of that the first time he'd kissed her…and it had scared him silly. After holding her again, it was going to be an all-out fight to keep away from her.

"Well, don't just stand there gawking at each other, say something," Esther Mae yelled from the bleachers, drawing Pace's gaze from Sheri.

Only then did he realize that they'd drawn the crowd's full attention. Esther Mae and Norma Sue were grinning as if they'd won a jackpot, and Miss Adela was just smiling her serene smile.

He looked back at Sheri and noticed she'd taken a few steps back. Her gaze darted from him to the posse.

Like a cassette tape dragging on low batteries Sheri's words droned in his head. *I need a boyfriend.* That's what she'd said two short weeks ago. His mouth went dry, his gaze narrowed on her.

He'd been had.

If he needed any more proof, all it took was another glance up at the posse congratulating themselves on their latest match.

She'd done what she'd set out to do, whether he'd consented or not. And if there was one thing Pace was not, it was somebody's fool.

He leveled his gaze on her. "So this is what all this has been about. I should have known." It took all his self-control, of which he had a considerable amount, to simply tip his hat to her and walk away.

Sheri had one of those moments. The kind that come after the fact. The kind that a person replayed over and over again in her head.

If only you'd listened!

Well, she hadn't listened and now she was seeing scorn like she'd never seen from anyone in the eyes of the cowboy she'd just kissed. She fidgeted as the corner of his lip curled and his left eyebrow followed the upward motion and cocked sarcastically.

He didn't say anything, but he said plenty.

You're a fool, Sheri Marsh.

Then he spun and stalked out of the building.

Sheri glanced around, feeling self-conscious about

her actions and knowing that her plan had just blown up in her face. While the posse was up in the stands too far away to have seen the contempt in Pace's expression, the cowboys lining the fence had seen it all.

Okay, she was a fool.

There was nothing left to do but go after him. "What are y'all looking at?" she huffed then jogged after Pace. The cowboys were chuckling behind her. That just went to show that men could find the oddest things amusing.

"Pace, wait. Please," she called, catching him, jogging to keep up as he wove through the trucks toward his own.

"Lady, you're good. I've seen liars in my life, but you take the prize. I actually thought all this was real, when it was nothing but a setup." His mind was reeling, rifling through everything, every word, every moment. "The roof trick was really good. You must have thought you'd hit gold with that charade."

"No, that's not how it was." Sheri thought of how he'd helped her, and realized that no matter what she said he'd think she was lying. "Honestly."

"Honestly!" He yanked open his truck door and climbed in. "Do you even know what that word means?"

Sheri stood stock-still, the scorn in his eyes and his words like a slap across the cheek.

He dropped his arm out the open window, and she watched as he backed out of the parking space.

When he stopped and shifted to Drive she took a step toward his window. "Pace, listen—"

His steely gaze stopped her in her tracks. "Now, why would I ever do something like that again? You chose your path. I hope you got what you wanted, and you and yourself live happily ever after."

Then he was gone. He drove out of the parking lot leaving her standing alone in a swirl of dust.

your ranch? Somehow you've got to convince him that you're
going to make him an even bigger..."

They hadn't gone. He drove out of the driveway in
front of her searching the dark.

Chapter Nineteen

Sheri stormed into her house and slammed the door.
What was wrong with her? All the way home from the
rodeo she'd felt like such a loser. Had achieving her stupid
goal of fooling the posse been worth Pace's contempt?

Restlessly she paced the kitchen, then stormed back
out into the sunshine. A run would be great, but she
couldn't very well jog past Pace's house. There was no
way she wanted to chance seeing that expression on his
face again. It had been awful.

Dropping to her knees beside the flower bed beneath
the old oak tree she began yanking weeds. She felt so
hideous. So worthless. Her gaze fell on the fat ceramic
frog nestled beside the marigolds. His lips were puckered and the sign around his neck read, Toads Need
Love, Too. She was the toad. Who would ever love her?
She closed her eyes and felt the sting of tears. She was
so ashamed...so empty.

Pace Gentry made her feel things she'd not ever felt

before. He was an honorable man trying to walk a life that would please God. He saw things so clearly. He was the type of man that would do whatever it took to make good on his word. And he expected nothing but the same from those around him.

He'd told her that in the very beginning when she'd first approached him about pretending to be her boy-friend. Yet she'd taken advantage of his proximity knowing full well she was going against his belief and moral code.

For what? To play games with a group of ladies who in the end really only had her best interests at heart.

Sheri grabbed a bitter weed and yanked.

So what are you going to do about it?

The voice was a soft whisper on the wind. Her con-science digging into her. What could she do? Go beg Pace to forgive her? Why? The man had lost all respect for her, so what did it matter? What good would it do?

Her weeding forgotten she stared through the tree branches to the blue sky beyond. "This is a fine mess I've gotten myself into."

Pace said God expected his people to be salt and light to the world. Sheri admired the way he'd left a life he loved behind to try and do what God expected of him. Lacy had done the same thing. Some would look at Sheri and think she'd been so noble to come to Mule Hollow. But she wasn't. She'd come to Mule Hollow because she didn't have anything better to do.

What did God expect of her?

She'd never asked herself that question before. She simply lived her life as if she had a free ride or something. Like everyone else was expected to strive for a life pleasing to the Lord, but she'd been excused from stepping up.

Well, Pace had stepped up. He stood for something. He was honorable, loved God with all his heart, and was trying to prove it by doing what God expected of him. He was trying to become an even better man. And she'd not only disappointed him, she'd tried to compromise everything he stood for.

For the first time in her life, Sheri really looked at herself. Was that who she wanted to be? No wonder she felt like the Lord had forgotten her. What had she done for Him? Lacy had come to Mule Hollow to do a ministry. Pace had come to show the Lord he was willing to give up a life he loved, go against his love of solitude and be a witness. But what had she done? Literally. What had she done for the Lord? But also what had she done to Pace? She had to find a way to fix this. She knew the first step was to ask the Lord to forgive her.

And then to find a way to get Pace to do the same.

Pace was coming out of the round pen leading his horse when he saw Sheri standing beside the gate. He strode past her without saying a word. He ignored the lost look he saw in her eyes. He'd never felt as betrayed as he had at the end of that very public kiss. To some it might have seemed a small thing; if he couldn't trust a person then he had no use for them. He didn't trust Sheri. The fact that he'd wanted to cut deep.

"Pace. Talk to me."

She followed him to the barn as he stripped the mare

down and started brushing her. His thoughts had been full of Sheri all afternoon even though he'd told himself to forget about her.

"I'm sorry," she said. There was none of her usual sassiness in her tone. He almost believed her, but then he thought about the roof and what an actress she was. He hardened his heart to his yearning to believe her.

"Well, I don't blame you for not believing me, but I needed to come and tell you that I am sorry for what I did."

He heard her turn and move toward the door. His hand stilled its brushing, the impulse strong to call her back. He kept silent and let her go.

She stopped at the door, but he kept his back to her. He thought she was going to say something else, but after a pause she continued on her way. It was just as well.

He resumed brushing down the horse. After all, he'd come to Mule Hollow with a purpose. Sheri wasn't a part of that purpose. Instead she'd distracted him.

It was time to get on with things.

It was time to forget Sheri Marsh.

"Miss. Where's the bathroom?"

Sheri looked up from the sink, tears streaming down her cheeks thanks to the onions she was chopping, to find a girl of about thirteen jogging toward her with an anxious look on her face.

"Second door on the right." Sheri swiped her eyes with the back of her hand and pointed the knife she was holding down the hallway of Cort and Lilly's home. She'd been directing traffic of some sort from the moment she'd arrived an hour earlier.

When Lilly had asked her out of the blue to help with the youth retreat they were holding at their house, Sheri's first reaction had been a flat no. Then she'd remembered that she'd been praying for the Lord to show her some way He could use her. It had been three weeks since she'd tried to use Pace. Three weeks since she'd lost his respect. Three long weeks of searching for answers and absolution.

She'd seen very little of her neighbor. He'd kept busy down the road from her, and she'd stopped jogging past his house. It was surprising how easy it was to avoid each other.

But Sheri had accepted Lilly's plea to help out, and that meant she'd decided to stop avoiding Pace. Since he and Cort had come up with this idea, seeing him was inevitable.

She'd thought she could handle it. Now, she was fighting her nerves, and it wasn't all because of Pace. She hadn't realized that the place would literally be swarming with kids. She had barely come in the front door when Lilly had waved her into the kitchen and set her to chopping onions. That was a good thing. At least she wasn't having to deal with the kids one-on-one.

She wasn't good with kids, had never pretended to be and wasn't real certain kids were her calling. That didn't mean she didn't like kids. She did. It was just, well, they might ask her a question she didn't have an answer to. Worse, what if she gave them the wrong answer? With her big mouth she could do irreparable damage. She wasn't proud of that. After what she'd done to Pace she'd thought more than once that Lilly had lost her mind inviting her to be a helper on this shindig. There were plenty of others who would have been far better choices than her.

"Earth to Sheri. Are you in there?"

"Oh, sorry, I got lost thinking." Sheri gave Lilly a sheepish grin while she rinsed her hands off.

"Sheri, please relax. I can't believe how nervous you seem. I've been watching you, and every time that door opens you jump."

Sheri started placing hot dogs on a large platter in preparation for the roast they were going to have as soon as the sun went down. She glanced around to make certain there was no one around to hear her. "To tell you the truth, kids make me nervous."

Lilly's eyes grew wide. "No way."

"It's true. See, I have a secret. I'm full of a lot of hot air. I rarely actually know what I'm talking about."

"So you're telling me that the snappy Sheri, with an answer for everything, has an Achilles' heel?"

"If that's what you call it. Yeah."

Lilly paused in the middle of opening a package of buns and chuckled, her dark ringlets dancing. "So that's why Lacy was grinning so big when she suggested I ask you to help me."

"So that's how you chose me. I've been had. The way I see it, a kid's brain is a terrible thing to waste, and I'd hate to be wasteful when any and all advice I give is basically a salad toss."

"And what is that supposed to mean?"

"It means I don't have the instinct that mothers have. It means that I have a goofed-up head myself, and I'd hate to pass that on to some poor unsuspecting kid."

"Sheri, you are talking to the woman who was raised by a herd of man-hating grannies. If you want to hear some oddball advice then you've come to the right place. But you know what I've found out?"

"What?"

"That no one has all the right answers. You'll be fine. Anyway, the two chaperones are here to watch out for them and answer any life-altering questions they may choose to spring on us. Our job is to provide meals and clean up."

"Oh, that's a relief."

Lilly smiled. "I think that one of these days when you get married and have kids of your own you'll be wonderful. You learn with them, you know."

"I won't have to worry about that. I'm not getting married. No kids of my own in my future."

Lilly paused, holding the plastic bag of buns to her chest. "You can't be serious?"

"Sure I can."

Lilly looked at her as if she'd lost her mind. "But Sheri, you'd be great with kids. And Pace would be a great dad. I was watching him earlier, when he was introducing his horse to the group. They were mesmerized by him. Did you know his horse does the most amazing tricks?"

Sheri was speechless. She was relieved when the young girl burst out of the bathroom and raced past them, giving her a moment to collect her thoughts. The screen door slamming spurred Sheri out of her shock. "Lilly, I'm sure Pace will be a good father, if he chooses to marry and have kids one day. But me…we… There's nothing there." Where had Lilly been for the last three weeks?

"You are telling me that you don't have an interest in that *to-die-for* cowboy out there in our round pen?"

Sheri laid the last dog on the platter very carefully. She couldn't lie. She was done with all that so she spoke straightforwardly. "I'd be lying if I said I hadn't thought about it. But it can't ever happen. Please, please tell me this isn't a setup—that the posse isn't still scheming to get us together."

Lilly turned pink. "Mmmm, *well*—they told me they'd hoped the two of you would work out whatever has come between you. They hoped this weekend might help you. But don't get mad," she added hurriedly. "They just want to fix things."

Sheri started laughing. Truly, had she really expected any less?

"It doesn't matter," she said, her laughter dying away. "There is nothing between me and Pace," she said as wistfulness rolled through her. "At least nothing of value, and the sooner the posse understands that the better." She dropped the empty hot dog wrapper into the trash and let the lid drop with a thud.

There was nothing anyone could do. Pace Gentry was no fool. It was Sheri who had been the fool, and who knew that better than she did?

Chapter Twenty

Pace watched as the kids clamored around the picnic table with their straightened-out clothes hangers, hurrying to get their hot dog on the stick and join in the fun around the campfire. More like bonfire! Cort had built the thing so that it lit up the entire night sky as it burned. Standing in the shadows just out of reach of the glow, Pace searched for Sheri among the crowd. Coming up empty, he was surprised at the wave of disappointment that settled over him.

He'd kept busy in the weeks since he and Sheri had words. She'd stopped jogging past his place. Despite everything that had happened, he'd noticed her absence, and despite everything he'd missed her.

Glancing around at the kids he was amazed that he was here. When Cort had approached him to help with some weekend youth retreats that he'd set up, Pace had thought he'd lost his mind. Cort had pressed him, convinced that Pace would be great giving riding pointers to the kids. Pace had been hesitant at first. Then the Lord reminded him of why he'd left Idaho, and he'd accepted. This was his opportunity to use his love of horses as a bridge to interact with a group of kids. It was an opportunity to be a witness for Christ.

He'd already committed to helping when he learned that Sheri had come on board. Since he'd already given Cort his word there was no backing out. No avoiding her. And despite the gulf that was between them, there was a deep part of him that wanted to see her. Over the weeks he'd only seen her at church at a distance. They'd both been careful to steer clear of each other. Even though there had been a few times when it was plain that the ladies were trying hard to connect them, Sheri obviously was determined not to come near him. As soon as Norma Sue would call him over to their group Sheri would head to her Jeep.

The Lord had been after him for the last week to try and set things right between them. After all, she'd apologized, and he'd sent her away. She'd basically asked for forgiveness and he'd shunned her. Every time he'd picked up his Bible since then he somehow managed to read passages on forgiving your neighbor. God was sending him a message, but as of yet he'd been too stubborn to submit.

She'd lied to him. She'd tried to use him. The odd thing was that the posse didn't seem to care one way or the other that they'd been deceived. They knew what had happened. Roy Don told him that Sheri had called a meeting at Roy and Norma Sue's house and explained everything and asked them to forgive her for being so conniving. Obviously they'd done the right thing. They'd forgiven her.

So he had a dilemma. He needed to accept her apology and move on, and a part of him wanted that more than he could begin to understand. It was that part that had him running scared.

Sheri stepped into view carrying a tray of hot dogs. The moment he glimpsed her his heart kicked up a notch. Everything around him charged up the way it did just before he stepped into the stirrup of a bronc. In many ways Sheri reminded him of a wild bronc...so full of turns and contradictions that it was a struggle to keep up with her.

She had on faded jeans, her red boots and a tank top. He smiled automatically when she raised her eyes and their gazes melded together.

She had a hold on him. *But she disappointed him.*

In the flicker of the fire, shadows danced along her silhouette and time seemed to stand still. In that moment he made a decision. He was duty bound to accept her apology. He'd do it then be able to move on, to stop thinking about her. He took a step, then wove through the kids to get to her. She watched him all the way. When he stood a foot in front of her he had the urge to touch her. He shoved the urge away and got to the point.

"We need to talk."

Sheri had been startled when she'd found Pace staring at her. When he'd stormed through the group of kids toward her she'd felt as she had the day she'd caused him to get tossed off the mustang. The man had a glint in his eye and a purpose in his step that was formidable. In the flickering firelight he looked as if he was bearing down on an outlaw.

It was intimidating, but she refused to be intimidated by him anymore. True, she'd been in the wrong using him as she'd done. But she'd apologized, and if he couldn't accept it then so be it. He for certain wasn't going to throw demands at her.

"Talk," she said, stepping away from the group of girls whose mouths were hanging open looking up at Pace. She wasn't sure if they were scared of him or enthralled by him. It was probably a little of both. "I've got things to do, cowboy." Lifting her chin she stalked toward the house to get more food. In a flash, Sheri's irritation had flared out of control. The man wanted to talk, and she'd been wanting to talk, so why was she suddenly so angry with him?

"I'll help you," he said, falling into step beside her.

"No thanks," she huffed and walked faster. "I'm fine on my own."

They reached the back door. She went to open the screen but he threw his hand over her shoulder and held the door closed. She yanked hard then twisted around to glare up at him. Suddenly finding herself practically in his embrace, she stepped back and pressed her back against the door. "Why'd you do that?" she snapped, frustrated by his nearness. His scent enveloped her, the smell of leather and soap. It was a very distracting and appealing scent and one she'd missed.

"I need to talk to you," he said slowly. His eyes were dark, and his brows dipped below the rim of his hat.

"That's a little awkward. Don't you think?"

"What does that mean? And what is wrong with you?"

"Me? What's wrong with me? I come and apologize to you, and you turn me away like I've committed the unpardonable sin, when I was doing the right thing. Then, you make no attempt to talk to me for three weeks and all of a sudden you practically *demand* to talk to me." She knew she was overreacting, but telling herself to calm down was like talking to…well it was like talking to Pace Gentry—a hardheaded goat! As a matter of fact, if he wanted to talk then he would get a piece of her mind. "And another thing! If you think I'm going to grovel to get your forgiveness, well, you have another think coming, cowboy."

He stepped back and yanked his hat off his head. His dark hair was plastered across his forehead as he rammed a hand through it and stared at her. "I don't expect that," he said.

The softness in his voice set her back. She felt a little, just a little embarrassed as she shifted her weight from one boot to the other. "Well. What do you expect?"

"I guess, what I was thinking is maybe we could start over. After you accept my apology for holding you to a higher standard than I was willing to meet myself."

Well, at least that was a start. "I don't think so," she said. "I haven't gotten the posse to completely give up on the idea of you and me being meant for each other. If they were to see us start speaking to each other it'd just rile them up again. I mean, knowing we agree that things between us are okay would be nice to know. But that'd be all."

He slapped his hat on his thigh, his expression grim.

"So would it be all that bad if they thought there might be something to this notion of theirs that we might be right for each other?"

Sheri's heart stopped beating. Just stopped for an insane moment as something she didn't recognize flared inside of her. "It wouldn't be fair to anyone. Especially you," she said, shaking off the odd feeling.

"I don't understand."

"Look, Pace." She figured it was time to just lay it all out there for him and be done with it once and for all. "Nothing has changed for me. I'm still not planning on marrying. I've got too much baggage from my past to risk it. With the way my parents were, and the way I am, there's still a chance that I couldn't one hundred percent commit to one man for the rest of my life. Not that I'm saying that's even something you might consider wanting with me. But I'm just thinking that you should know this."

He scowled. "I'm not asking you to marry me. I'm just asking you out."

She hadn't really thought he might be thinking marriage, so why did his statement hurt so much? She lifted her chin. "I don't think so. I'm trying to figure out some things right now," she said with force, as much to convince herself as Pace.

"Like what?"

She studied him. "Like why am I here. I've been so busy running from who I am that I don't really know myself anymore. And I want to know. God has a purpose for me. As mixed up as I am, He made me, so there's got to be a reason."

Pace reached out suddenly and ran his finger down

her jaw, rattling her. "You're a wonderful woman, Sheri. I know God has great plans for you, but I still don't get why you're so dead set against ever getting married."

She stepped away from his touch; it distracted her more than she could take. "I realized something was really wrong with the sense of accomplishment I get from watching everyone else's dreams come true. I figured out that is exactly the problem—they're everyone else's dreams. It's time for me to find my own."

He slammed his hat on, and she could see the frustration in the set of his jaw. Why was he so frustrated?

"That's all well and good. But why can't your dreams include marriage?"

Now she was frustrated again. "I don't get why it matters to you so much, but if you must know—I'd never take a chance on getting married and having kids and dragging them through anything like what I went through growing up."

"Why would you think you'd do something like that to your kids? You wouldn't. Looks to me like you need to start believing in yourself a little more."

Sheri's head was starting to spin. Couldn't the man hear? "Well, that's what I've been saying."

"No, if that's what you'd been saying then you'd have enough sense to know that you'd be a great mother." His expression was so intense that for an instant he had her believing him. Or at least wanting to believe him, but she didn't.

"That just shows how little you know about me. Look, I need to get the stuff for s'mores before there's a stampede."

He studied her for a moment, then reached over her shoulder and opened the door. She slipped around the edge of it, her nerves jangling when he followed. She wanted him to go away.

Really needed him to go.

The last thing she needed was for him to make her wish for something she knew she'd never allow herself to have.

And that was exactly what was happening.

Chapter Twenty-One

Sheri gave up on sleep at 5:00 a.m. and crept into the kitchen to make a pot of coffee.

It had been a wild night in a house full of young girls. All the guys including Pace, Cort, Ron and the youth pastor who had brought the kids, were bunking down the lane at the house that had been Lilly's when she and Cort had married.

Sheri hadn't realized how lively ten-to-twelve-year-olds could be. Though she'd been told that she didn't have to stay up with them she'd known being alone after her disturbing encounter with Pace wasn't what she'd needed. So she'd stayed up and had a great time.

They'd sung and partied well past two in the morning. Once the girls realized she was a nail tech they'd whipped more polish than she had in her salon from their overnight bags and begged her to do manicures and pedicures. She'd been more than happy to oblige them, and for a few hours was able to derail thoughts of Pace.

But, no sooner than when everyone had finally sacked out sometime near three in the morning, did the thoughts of Pace roll in like the heavy fog.

Realizing the futility in trying to sleep, the lure of coffee and some sort of sweet comfort food drew her to Lilly's kitchen and Lilly's stash of banana taffy. Thankfully, Sheri knew where it was kept. Moving quietly around the kitchen she prepared the coffeemaker then lifted the lid off the large tin container that sat beside the back door. Inside was the chewy treat that Lilly and Samantha, Lilly's donkey, had a huge weakness for. Normally a chocolate girl herself, Sheri wasn't going to be choosy right now. She grabbed a handful of taffy and was ripping into a piece when a bumping noise drew her attention to the window beside the door.

"Ohhh!"

She almost dropped everything before realizing that the eyeball peering in at her belonged to Samantha. While Sheri recouped her calm and thanked the Lord that she hadn't screamed so loud she'd awakened the entire house, Samantha drew her blinking eye away from the windowpane, squished her nose and bulbous lips against the glass and pressed. The end result was what looked like velvet lips ringing gigantic teeth in a very odd smile.

It was then she understood Samantha had gotten a glimpse of the yellow candy in her hand and was hinting that she would enjoy sharing.

Despite her heavy heart Sheri chuckled. She quickly poured herself a cup of coffee, grabbed the candy and went outside to join the nosy animal on the porch.

"Hey, Samantha, how's it going, girlfriend?" She held out the already unwrapped piece of taffy, holding her palm flat as she'd seen Lilly do, and watched as the roly-poly burro placed her lips to her palm and very daintily picked up the treat. This animal was almost human, Sheri thought as she started walking and Samantha trotted beside her happily smacking away.

It was a lovely warm early morning and Sheri decided to walk. She carried her coffee and candy across the large gravel drive to the stables where she'd seen a double swing sitting. She eased down and sipped her coffee.

Not-to-be-forgotten Samantha stood beside her, eyeing the pocket that contained the taffy.

"Hey, stop eyeing the goodies. You're still smacking on your first piece." She had to laugh when the burro swallowed with a gulp then puckered her lips indicating it was time for another.

"Ya little piglet. You're getting a little round on the sides there, ya know." Samantha just blinked, as if to say that there were just some things in life worth sacrificing a good figure for. Sheri had to admit that the taffy was growing on her, too.

Tucking her feet beneath her, she set her cup on the armrest as she unwrapped two pieces of candy for each of them. A few seconds later, to the melodious sound of Samantha's smacking, Sheri stared out at the horizon and the thin thread of light separating night from morning. It reminded her of the morning Lacy dragged her to watch the mustangs arrive. The morning she met Pace. The morning her troubles began.

Today, there was a soft mist hovering over the ground

where the pasture sloped away from the yard. Sheri felt herself relax, lost in a sleepy daydream.

She'd recently watched the movie version of Jane Austen's classic romance, *Pride and Prejudice*. It wasn't an old Western, but she'd really enjoyed it. Thinking about it now, she realized Pace reminded her of Mr. Darcy with his quiet ways. The thought brought a tired smile to her lips. Not much of a reader she was a bit behind the curve, having never read the book. Over the years she'd heard comments about Mr. Darcy and she'd envisioned an older man with graying hair who was the butler or something. Not until the movie did she realize that Mr. Darcy was the handsome hero, prone to bouts of clipped words and a seemingly harsh attitude. But really, once you got past that he was actually magnificently wonderful.

Just like Pace.

In one of the most beautiful and romantic scenes of cinematography Sheri had ever admired, Mr. Darcy was filmed walking across the moors. Wearing a billowing white shirt, dark riding pants and boots, he advanced through the morning mist, appearing as if the heroine had dreamed him in her longing to see him. Now, sitting here watching the early dawn's mist glisten in the soft glow of light, Sheri's eyes felt heavy and she found herself watching and wishing that Pace would come. She could see Pace, tall and handsome, his hat off, his hair swept back from his face as if he'd been running his hands through it restlessly waiting for morning's light so that he could follow his heart to her.

Sheri's heartbeat drummed at the base of her neck as

ridiculously she strained to find Pace in the mist. Of course, it was only a movie and a make-believe hero. Sheri blinked and looked away from the horizon to the empty coffee cup she held limply in her hand. She hadn't even remembered drinking the coffee she'd been so lost in her imaginings.

She closed her eyes reliving the look in Pace's eyes when he'd asked her to start over...

And her heart wished it could.

"Don't touch her, Frankie."

"I wasn't gonna. Do you think she slept out here?"

"What happened to her hair?"

"What's the big deal? That's how my mom looks when she wakes up in the morning."

"Ick. You mean you gotta look at that every day?"

"That's how moms look. You get used to it."

Sheri was dreaming. In her dream she could hear boys talking but couldn't see what they were talking about. Groggily she rubbed her eyes, stretched and rolled over on the small twin bed, settling in for a little longer. Funny she hadn't remembered the bed being so small and bumpy.

"Hey, guys, what are y'all looking at?"

Sheri jumped, recognizing Pace's voice as she rolled off her bed. She woke with a start lying facedown in the grass staring at a pair of scuffed cowboy boots with exaggerated silver spurs.

"I guess it goes without saying that you didn't have a good night," Pace drawled from above her.

Looking up, Sheri found herself gazing into his

laughing eyes. He was flanked by six ten-year-old boys who were gawking at her as if she were an alien from another planet. If she looked as bad as she felt then it was pretty nightmarish.

Her mouth was so dry she knew she'd been sleeping on the swing with it wide open. Swallowing hard, she blinked and wished she could sink into a hole and disappear. It took her a moment to remember why she was even outside.

"Okay, the show's over. Move 'em out, boys."

"Sure thing, Mr. Pace," one boy said, turning to leave but stopping to grin back at him. "But you gotta admit it was way funny finding her lying asleep out here with her mouth hanging open like that."

"Yeah," crooned another one. "Man, I wonder if she swallowed any bugs."

Sheri choked.

Pace smiled down at her and held out a hand. "Come on, you can get up now."

She took the offered hand and let him pull her up off the ground. Instantly remembering the weird vision she'd had as the pleasant thrill of Pace's touch brought thoughts of Mr. Darcy crossing through the mist.

She tried to pull her hand free the moment she was on her feet.

"No," he said, holding her hand securely then tugging her within inches of him. Unlike her, he was freshly showered and smelled so good she wanted to lean in and just breathe him in, all zesty and fresh. Instead she tugged her hand harder and stepped away from him when he released it.

His smile said he knew exactly what she was doing. Just as she suspected he'd known exactly what he'd been doing when he'd tugged her so close and held her hand so long. *What was he up to now?*

Had the man not heard a word she'd said last night? She'd laid everything out clearly and he looked and acted as if nothing had happened.

"Cute outfit," he said, his smoky gaze drifting down her, humor lacing his words.

Sheri looked down and realized she was wearing her smiley-face cotton pajama pants and a bright yellow sleeveless T-shirt. "Funny man," she snapped, irritated. "What time is it?"

"It's seven, grumpy. The guys wanted to come down and get a head start riding the horses before breakfast. If I'd known we'd find you here I'd have come earlier."

"Breakfast! I need to go help Lilly," she gasped, thankful she had someplace to be instead of here. Pace was barking up the wrong tree if he thought she was going to change her mind about what she'd said. It didn't matter that she'd hardly slept, or even if she managed to eat a bug. Or that she'd gotten all mushy with her lack of sleep. Mr. Darcy, indeed! What had she been thinking?

She had a job to finish here, and then she had a path to find. The only way that path was going to include Pace was if God changed her DNA.

And she didn't see that happening.

She could never trust herself not to follow in the footsteps of her parents.

* * *

After a rowdy breakfast they took the kids on a hayride. It was the first one that Sheri had ever been on so she was as excited as the kids, even with the strain of her confrontation with Pace hanging over her head.

Determined to get her head back on straight she'd refocused her energies on the opportunity she'd been given to be around the group of youths. She'd actually relaxed about being around them now. Everything changed when she'd been painting the zillions of sets of toes and fingers they'd had her paint. It was really weird when she realized that instead of the girls being scared off, they were actually seeking her out. She didn't guard herself around them and she thought that might have been part of why they liked her.

By the time everyone loaded onto the hay-covered flatbed trailer that Cort was pulling behind his tractor, Sheri was more than ready to sink into the soft hay surrounded by a gaggle of giggling girls.

Lilly had the most beautiful singing voice Sheri had ever heard and soon had everyone joining in as they rode along through the pastures. Cort drove them through freshly-mowed hay fields and along the perimeter of a large tree-shrouded pond.

The kids spotted several animals along the way, including a rattlesnake. When one of the boys pointed it out all the girls screamed, including Sheri. She hated snakes and had no problem admitting it. Pace was sitting at the back of the trailer with Pastor Ron and was able to calm everyone's fears.

The man had no trouble getting the kids' attention.

When he spoke everyone listened, and he was good with them. Sheri was a little surprised at that. But why shouldn't they like him? She watched him with interest as he explained to the group that they were too far away for the snake to harm them, but that it was a good reminder to be careful when they were out and about. Very quickly the boys started asking Pace questions about his life as a cowboy. One question led to another and soon they had him telling stories about living alone out in the deserted country. Sheri wondered if he even realized how easily he was interacting with the kids.

Despite her need to distance herself from thinking about him, Sheri was mesmerized, as usual, listening to Pace talk about his past. Who wouldn't be? He'd been right in following the path he felt the Lord had called him to seek out. He could be a great influence.

The hayride turned into a lesson in respecting nature. It was obvious he still missed his Idaho and that he loved the wilderness of the Great Basin. Goodness, listening to him talk she wanted to go live in a shack in the vast wilderness herself.

He had an endearing way of telling about his many adventures that drew a person to listen to what he had to say. Sheri was not surprised by the way the kids on the trailer hung on his every word.

He'd come to Mule Hollow looking to be used by God, looking to move out of his comfort zone and reach for something he couldn't see but that he knew God wanted him to go after. Sheri admired him for what he'd done, and she had a sense of pride knowing that his dream was going to come true. God was already using him and she knew in her heart that this was only the beginning. .

Sheri's longing to find God's path in her life grew watching Pace. God had a plan for her life, and she had finally decided she was going to seek it out. The Bible said, "Seek and ye shall find." Well, she was going to do just that, and she wasn't going to let anything stop her.

Chapter Twenty-Two

❧

Pace was about to enter Sam's Diner when Cassie almost ran over him plowing through the swinging door.

"Hey, Pace, you're late. The lunch crowd already left. Lucky for you Sam's still got some food in there." She stopped on the sidewalk and smiled up at him. She was a baby-faced kid, and Pace had to remind himself she was almost twenty and not the sixteen she looked to be.

"I wanted to tell you thank you," she said.

"For what?"

"For teaching Jake. He's really enjoying working with you."

"He's doing me a favor helping out and he's a fast learner. I'm proud to have him helping me." He was. "He tells me you're thinking about taking some college courses over in Ranger."

"Yes, sir. I want to take some business courses."

"Sounds like a plan to me."

"Yeah, a girl needs a plan. Well, I gotta run. Watch out in there. Sam's grumpy."

What else was new? Sam was grumpy all the time these days. "What's wrong now? Did someone stick a nickel in the jukebox?"

Cassie shook her head. "No, it's about Adela. For a smart man he's real dense. I told him he needs to just do it. Ask her to marry him and live happily ever after."

"And what did he say?"

Cassie jogged down the steps and opened the door of her compact car. "Actually, he surprised me by saying he was thinking about it." She paused before sitting down. "Of course, as slow as he thinks, it could be next year before he makes a decision. Someone needs to go in there and give him a push."

Pace watched her drive off then strode inside. He'd come to a decision himself concerning Sheri. He'd prayed hard about it during the week since the youth retreat. He was going to pursue Sheri Marsh whether she wanted him to or not. He'd come to realize that he had never felt the way he felt when he was around her. She brightened his day when she was near, and he thought about her all the time. He'd tried to give her some space, but it was starting to drive him crazy knowing she was within a stone's throw from him and he couldn't spend time with her. She was almost all he thought about. He'd given the whole issue over to the Lord, and he was trusting the Lord to show him the way. He wondered as he saw Sam busy behind the counter if Sam was trusting the Lord.

"Hi, Sam," he said and called out a louder greeting

to Applegate and Stanley, not certain if they had their hearing aids on.

"Afternoon, Pace," Sam said, slapping his dish towel across his shoulder. "I hear ya had a right nice little campout for that church group out at Cort's place."

"Yes, sir. It was real good." Pace took a seat at the counter and nodded when Sam held up the coffeepot. "Sam, can I tell you something?" He glanced over toward Applegate and Stanley, but they were caught up in their game.

Sam set Pace's coffee on the counter and nodded. "Sure ya can. Don't mind them two. Is somethin' troublin' ya?"

"When I came to Mule Hollow a month ago, I didn't know what to expect. You know how I loved living out in Idaho."

Sam snorted. "Yep, I know. Took guts to do what you did."

"That's what I wanted to talk about. Everybody thinks that, but I have to confess I didn't have the guts everyone is giving me credit for. I had a backup plan all along." He fiddled with his cup. "See, I figured that if I kept certain options open, didn't tie myself down, if things didn't work out I'd be free to head back up to Idaho."

"Nothin' wrong with that," Sam said, wiping down the counter.

"Except that I'm a fraud. I had options, when everyone is patting me on the back for following God blindly into unknown territory."

Sam slapped the dish towel over his shoulder again and crossed his wiry arms. "I still don't see what's wrong with that. You took action. That's more'n most of us can boast."

Pace nursed his coffee and thought about how to proceed, then just trusted the Lord. "See, Sam. What I'm trying to say is that all that's changed now. I really enjoyed giving those kids hands-on experience with horses, and I had the opportunity to speak to a few of them about the Lord."

"Sounds like you might be hatching a plan for a future."

Pace nodded slowly. "This is where it gets tricky. It's more than realizing I might be able to make a difference in a kid's life. It's about Sheri, too."

Sam's expression changed. "Oh, boy."

Pace chuckled. "That's exactly what I said. I fought it for the first few weeks. But I figured out this weekend that I came here looking for God's plan for my life, and suddenly I was limiting Him."

"What do you mean?" Sam had started drying cups from a pan but his hands stilled.

"It means I'm giving God total control now."

"And that means Sheri?"

Pace smiled. "Yes, or at least I'm going to give it a chance."

Sam looked around the diner. "I've lived my life inside these walls, watching everybody else living their lives out there. Kinda partaking through them. I admire you for what yer doin', Pace. What does Sheri say about all of this?"

"She basically told me to get lost."

"That figures," Sam snorted. "She ain't one to mince words, and I never took her for one set on settling down."

"I think she doesn't have enough faith in herself and in God. And I think I'm here to give her a hand with that."

Sam put both hands on the counter. "That's a tough one. I know 'cause I hate to admit it but I'm living it myself."

Pace had opened up to Sam wondering if the Lord would use the conversation. Now he prayed that he'd continue to have the words Sam needed.

"How's that?"

"I've been a bachelor all my life. I fell in love with Adela the first time I saw her. We were just kids, but her heart already belonged to Theo Ledbetter. I figure Theo was the luckiest man on earth to have had the privilege of being loved all his life by Adela and to have her as his wife."

"But Theo's been dead for years."

"Nearly sixteen years," Applegate yelled from the window.

So much for his hearing aid being turned off, Pace thought. "I never understood why the two of you haven't married."

"A man's got to ask before a woman can say yes," Stanley called and Pace decided the two men had a pretty good racket going by pretending they didn't hear what was happening around them. They had selective hearing loss.

"Well, that's true enough," Sam added, glaring at his two friends.

"Why haven't you asked?"

"Might as well admit the truth, Sam," Applegate said. "You can't be helped until ya admit ya got a problem. Ain't that right, Stanley?"

"Yep—"

"Fear," Sam snapped, cutting Stanley off. "I'm a blamed ole coward. There. Are you two old goats satisfied?"

Pace looked from one to the other. "But it's obvious she loves you and more than apparent you love her."

"True. But, well, things are comfortable the way they are. I'm afraid to give up what I've got. If I were to try and change things…I might mess it all up."

Pace suddenly understood looking at the older man. He was clinging to what they had, rather than trying for something better. Like Pace had done clinging to his old life. Sam had to let go just as he'd had to do. "Sam, it looks like we have a lot in common."

"How's that?"

Pace met the little man's somber gaze with a smile of certainty. "What you've got to do is trust the Lord and give up your Idaho. Just like I did."

Chapter Twenty-Three

"Ohh! Oooohhh, that tickles!"

"Esther Mae, you have to hold still if you want this to look right."

"I know, but I am so ticklish."

"I'm sorry, but I can't get these stripes straight if you jump every time I touch your toes."

"Yeah, Esther Mae," Norma Sue said from where she stood looking over Sheri's shoulder. She'd been hovering there ever since Sheri had begun painting a tiny American flag on Esther's big toenail. "Be still. Your flag's waving."

Esther Mae grabbed the chair arms in a grip that would have challenged Sam's handshake. "I'll try to sit still, but watch yourself. I might kick you without meaning to. If I can just get past being so ticklish I think I'm really going to like this nail art. It's such an expression of who I am. I think I want to try one of those cute rhinestone toe rings, too. Ohh!" she squealed, yanking her toe free of Sheri's grasp. "Sorry. Try it again."

"A toe ring!" Norma Sue exclaimed as Sheri reached for Esther Mae's toe one more time. This was going to be the weirdest-looking American flag she'd ever tried to paint on a toenail.

"That's right—a toe ring."

"Esther Mae," Norma Sue said, drawing the Mae out as if she were dragging it up a mountain. "You express yourself just fine. It's one thing to get doodads on your toenails, but a toe ring?"

"Norma Sue," Adela said softly from the styling chair where Lacy was finishing up her haircut, "I think it's nice the way Esther Mae is trying new things. Sometimes change is good."

Lacy whipped the cutting cape from around her neck. "Adela, you're a free woman," she said. "You know me, I think change is a great thing. I love it."

"Me, too," Esther Mae said, nodding. "Just because we're almost seventy is no reason we have to subject ourselves to boredom. Sheri, I *will* take one of those rings. The red one please. The brighter the better."

Norma Sue bopped her forehead with the palm of her hand. "Okay, okay, I give up. Who am I to try and make you give up your fun? Adela, you sure are quiet today."

"Are you feeling well?" Lacy asked and Sheri glanced toward them, catching the sudden sadness in Adela's eyes.

"Well, now that we're talking about change. All of you know that a few weeks ago my daughter asked me to move to Abilene."

Norma Sue snorted. "Yeah, that was the most ridiculous thing I ever heard."

"I've been praying about it. And I think I may go."

Heavenly Inspirations had never been as quiet as in that moment. Sheri was so shocked by the announcement she almost dropped the bottle of white polish. Adela moving—it was inconceivable. Really, no one had even given it a second thought when Adela had mentioned it before. Mule Hollow without Adela? No way.

"But why?" Esther Mae whined, her toe ring forgotten. "You have a life here."

"Adela, why haven't you asked us to pray with you?" Leave it to Lacy to zero in on the spiritual need.

Adela, her beautiful blue eyes sad but sure, met each of their gazes one after the other. "You are my friends, and I just thought I should warn you of things to come. I didn't tell you earlier because I have no doubts the Lord is going to give me the right answer in His own time."

"The answer is no!" Norma Sue huffed, moving to stand beside her lifelong friend.

"That's right," Esther Mae agreed. "This is about Sam, isn't it? If the man would only come to his senses and marry you, then—"

Adela shook her head. "Esther Mae, this isn't about Sam. It's about practicality."

"Practicality, my foot!" Norma Sue snapped. "Nope, this is about love and you know it. You of all people, Adela, running. I can't believe it."

Sheri finished Esther Mae's toe, slid the red toe ring on her third toe, and listened to the conversation. All week long she'd awakened each morning and proceeded to force herself to put one foot in front of the other while telling herself all the practical reasons she should stop thinking about Pace. She was supposed to be figuring out what the Lord wanted her to do with her life, but she couldn't stop thinking about Pace and his dreams.

"Adela," Sheri said, picking up a slender cuticle stick and rolling it between her fingers. "Why don't you ask Sam to marry you?"

"Now there's an idea," Esther Mae gasped.

"Yeah, Adela." Lacy's eyes lit up. "You can't just give up on the man and leave him here. Just think about it. He'd be so sad and grumpy none of us would know what to do with him."

Adela blushed. "I couldn't do that. Besides, I've always trusted the Lord's timing. Me asking Sam would be rushing God's plan. This is something Sam has to work out for himself."

"Then leaving before God's plan happens wouldn't be right, either," Sheri pointed out, and everyone joined in talking at once agreeing with her.

"Come on, Adela, shake up the love boat," Lacy laughed. "Really, if you're going to leave anyway, what could it hurt? The verse I was reading this morning would be suited for you *and* for you, too, Sheri. It's from Second Timothy. 'God did not give us a spirit of timidity, but a spirit of power.' I think we need to see some of that power being utilized right now."

Sheri quirked an eyebrow at Lacy. "I'm getting there. But we're talking about Adela right now."

For the last few days, she'd talked with Lacy about how she'd been feeling about finding out what God's plan was for her life. And Lacy had been quick to point out that she was missing the boat by not believing that

God might have brought Pace into her life for a reason. Sheri wasn't completely sure about that. She wasn't willing to make a mistake when it came to Pace. She'd already caused him enough trouble. And while she might have begun to dream of a life with Pace, until she got the go-ahead from the Lord she felt the best thing was to keep her feelings to herself. Pushing aside thoughts of herself, she looked at Adela. She was sitting quietly studying her hands which were clasped tightly together in her lap. The short wispy white hair around her face hid her eyes from them.

Sheri remembered the first day she'd seen those eyes. Sheri had never seen more peaceful eyes in all of her life. They'd reminded her of Lacy's eyes, so blue and with that sparkle that Sheri felt certain came from a strong bond with the Lord. A bond Sheri had wished she could emulate. But she'd learned that while she could teach herself and command herself to walk through life emulating Lacy's vivaciousness, she couldn't command the Lord to have a relationship with her that she'd convinced herself was only for a privileged few like Adela and Lacy. And why not? They were special. They were the ones who came up with just the right verses to inspire people or spur them to action. They were the ones people like her imitated…just weeks ago she'd settled for that.

Now she knew that she could have the same kind of relationship with God. It was out there for everyone, all she had to do was seek Him with all her heart. That meant learning to walk with Him on a daily basis. It meant that she needed to study His word and hide it in her heart. It meant she needed to do a little work. She'd realized that while she was a Christian, she wasn't growing in her belief. Lacy and Adela had immersed themselves in God's word, seeking out His will.

Pace was doing the same thing. And she loved him because of it. It was true…he made her want to be the best person she could be. And though she had begun to dream of having a life with him it was better to stay out of his life for now. She still wasn't certain she could trust herself. Despite everything, her past still haunted her.

Adela was different. It killed Sheri to see her faltering and suddenly she knew she had to do something.

"Adela, you have to fight for what *you* want sometimes. You have fought for everyone else to have the happiness you thought they deserved all these months. Don't sit there and think for one moment I don't know that you haven't been instrumental in all these setups."

"That's the truth," Esther Mae said. "She's got your number on that, Adela."

"You are the one who thought this whole 'Wives Needed' campaign for Mule Hollow," Norma Sue added.

Lacy plopped her hands to her hips and cocked her shaggy head to the side. "You have to fight for the principle of it all. I mean really, Adela, come on. Let's go put Sam out of his misery."

Adela's eyes lit up, spurring Sheri on.

"You know you're not going to move away from here and leave all of us." Sheri walked to the door and opened it wide. Something inside of her was driven to see Adela fight for her right to a happily ever after. "Now come on, what do you say? It's a great day for a marriage proposal."

"You're gonna do it. You're really gonna do it!"

"Hush, Applegate. Ya been after me for years to do this so let me do it."

"Right." Applegate stopped his hovering and stood still, watching as Sam yanked off his apron and dropped it to the counter, tugged the waistband of his britches up while tucking his shirttail in securely.

"You're right, Pace," he said. "There comes a time when turning back to the past ain't an option anymore. Ya gotta look to the future. If I don't do something to change her mind, my Adela is goin' ta load up and move off. Then where will I be? I'll be alone, regrettin' for the rest of my days that I didn't give up my fears and ask her to marry me."

"At's the way, Sam," Applegate said. "Here, slick yer hair down." He licked his palm and reached toward his friend's head. "When a man's goin' to ask a woman to be his wife he don't need a cowlick stickin' straight up off his crown. It ain't dignified."

"Get back, App!" Sam dodged Applegate's damp hand and headed toward the door with a determined stride with Applegate trailing behind.

Pace couldn't help chuckling. The two of them looked like a pair of overgrown kids as he and Stanley followed them out into the sunlight.

"Where is she, Sam?" Stanley asked.

"She's down at Lacy's getting her hair and nails done like she does every Friday at one o'clock."

"Then what are we waiting fer?" Applegate said, grinning. Applegate grinning—Pace figured that in itself was a miracle.

Sam cleared his throat, lifted his chin, and glanced from them down the street toward Lacy's. "Yer right, App. C'mon, time's a wastin'."

Sheri figured the Lord's timing was right on the money when she looked out that door to see Sam heading up the small parade marching down the center of Main Street. She almost got trampled in the stampede when she'd called everyone to come see.

One look and Norma Sue and Esther Mae whipped around and practically picked poor Adela up and scrambled out onto the sidewalk with her.

It was a sight. Sam, not quite five feet, looking as tall and determined as Pace Gentry, who was backing him up along with his sidekicks Applegate and Stanley.

Sheri had a great view of both Sam's and Adela's expressions as he came to a halt in front of Adela. If ever there were two people who loved each other it was these two. Sam slicked a hand from forehead to crown as Adela raised elegant, fine-boned fingers to touch a wisp of hair just behind her earlobe.

"Hello, Adela," he said, in a gentle voice that was reserved only for her.

"Hello, Sam," she answered, her voice a bit more breathy than usual.

Without further ado he dropped to his knee. "My sweet Adela. I've been a prideful man, but one who loves you more'n life itself. And if I ain't waited too long to get the gumption to ask you to marry me, then I'm askin' ya now. Will you do me the honor and be my wife?"

Sheri's heart swelled as a tear slid from the corner of her eye. It was so romantic. Adela took his face between her hands and looked deeply into his eyes.

"My Sam, my sweet Sam. I'd begun to think you were never going to ask. Yes. My answer is yes."

Sheri reacted by letting out a whoop. Everyone joined in, clapping as Sam sprang up and engulfed Adela in an embrace. Everyone was laughing and even Applegate Thornton was grinning like a hound dog getting a belly rub. Sheri figured this was a story for the weekly newspaper. It could go right there alongside Adela and Sam's wedding announcement.

Another wedding for Mule Hollow…. A wish tumbled through her and she closed her eyes, willing away the image that came of her and Pace.

"Can we talk?"

Now that just wasn't fair, she thought as she opened her eyes to find Pace standing half a step in front of her. Afraid to let him see what she'd been thinking, she'd avoided eye contact with him during Sam's proposal to Adela.

"Sure." And there you go—her mouth and her heart were giving her a mutiny! He started walking and she fell into step beside him, drawn to him despite the fact that she was willing her red frog giggers to run the other way.

"How have you been?"

So they were back to small talk. "Fine," she croaked. Her throat felt like a sandpit, while her heart was pounding. "Just fine."

They made it to the corner of Main Street and Pace turned left, along a sidewalk of empty buildings. And suddenly they were alone.

He smiled, coming to a halt. He turned and touched the hair at her temple and sent her already crumbling defenses into a freefall. She wanted to tell him that she loved him, but she couldn't, she had to learn to be a better person first. She had to get her life figured out first so that she wouldn't mess his up. But the look in his eyes was weakening her defenses.

"The Sheri Marsh I know wouldn't use the word fine. She'd use words like cool and awesome and kickin'. She would not say everything is fine. It's a dull dry word that is used when someone doesn't want to say that things are really boring or dull. Mundane."

She snapped her arms together across her chest and glared at him. She was trying to distance herself and he was standing there smiling at her, looking more handsome than any man had a right to look. It wasn't fair.

"How about a movie? Take me to a movie, Sheri."

The man was insufferable. He knew exactly what he was doing to her and he didn't care. Not one bit.

It was true she was tempted to throw caution to the wind and do it…but until she knew what God wanted from her she was not caving in. It was for his own good.

"No. I can't. Look, Pace, was there something other than this that you wanted to talk to me about?" There. She'd managed to sound firm and in control.

"No, Sheri, this is it. I want to talk to you about us." *Aww, man.* "There is no us."

"So when are you going to let there be? I've made up my mind I want you."

He wanted her! Sheri could have jumped for joy, instead she spun and stomped away from him. She had to put space between them. She wasn't ready.

"Sheri, you can't keep running away from this."

She swung around. "I am not running."

"Yes. You are. You're afraid."

He was right about that. "Look, Pace, I've been very vocal on the subject of marriage and the fact that I don't hang around very long. That does scare me. It should scare you."

"You can't speed-date forever."

Ha! "That's really none of your business. I already told you that I'm done with that, too."

"Sheri, you are not meant to live alone and you know it. You were really happy back there watching Sam and Adela."

"Well who wouldn't be happy that Sam finally asked Adela to get married? Of course I was happy. That has nothing to do with you deciding to, to—"

"To what? Try and finish what you started. To try and convince you that we're meant to be together like Adela and Sam."

"What I started was a ruse."

"No. What you started was a romance under the guise of a ruse. I think you know as well as I do that something bigger than both of us was happening from the moment we first butted heads."

Sheri crossed her arms and looked away from him because Mr. Smarty Buckaroo had a smug look in his gorgeous eyes and she didn't think she could hide her feelings from him too much longer if she kept looking at him. Oh, why was she even bothering?

"Okay." She met his smoky stare straight on. "Hope this makes you happy. It's true. I haven't ever felt like I feel when I'm around you. But, Pace, I can't count on it lasting. Take it from me, I know how I am. It may take a week, a month—hey, it could be a year or two, but in the end I'd be moving on. That's why I'm just calling it quits to all dating. I'm going to put all that energy into figuring out some kind of ministry I can do for the Lord. I'll never take a chance on marriage, kids and divorce." She knew it was true. Her past suddenly came rushing at her, reminding her of all the reasons she would never marry. "The quicker you understand that the better for both of us."

"So that's it? You're the last person I thought would accept defeat without a fight."

She took three strides and glared up at him. "There you go judging me again when you have no idea what's going on inside my head. You don't know what it felt like to be handed off like I was the family pet. You don't know what it felt like to have absolutely no control over any aspect of my life."

Pace stepped close to her, so close she could feel the warmth of him, but she was so overcome with the resentments she'd kept inside for so long that she couldn't move. She could only stare at the pockets of his shirt and battle the tears welling up inside her. She was breathing hard and when his arms went around her, to her horror, she crumpled against him. Just for a moment she let him hold her up. He was a tower of strength and for a minute she let herself go.

"Sheri, everything is going to be all right. You don't need to keep running. Don't you know that God's been with you all along? Talk to me, Sheri. Tell me what you want. What you really want. Stop being afraid." He stroked her hair, and she gripped his shirt tighter, felt his heart beating strong beneath her cheek.

She thought of Mr. Darcy striding across that moor. "I want the fairy tale! But I'm afraid."

"Of what?"

"Of me. I've told you that. Pace, I'll drag you through the mud because I can't trust that next week I'm not going to get bored—that I'm going to let you down."

"I'm not afraid of mud, Sheri."

"No."

"So you don't think our love is worth fighting for? Do you love me?" His voice was calm, patient, as it was with his horses. But his eyes were on fire, the steel-gray dark with emotions that seemed to glow like embers.

Sheri was nodding before she could stop herself. "Yes. Yes, I love you. I tried not to. I really did—but what do I know about love? Look what I came from."

He took her chin, traced his rough finger along her cheek in a sweet, tender manner. "You know, you need to start believing in yourself. In the goodness and the beliefs that run true inside of you. Sheri, you are strong. You don't have to pretend it—you are. Christ lives inside of you, Sheri, and if you'd just trust Him you'd be surprised at what He'll do. You couldn't control your life when you were a child left to the whims of your parents' foolishness. But you can control your choices now."

"I can't. I can't be certain yet, of myself."

"Yes, you can. Sheri, you have to stop letting your past be your crutch, or you're never going to be what God intended you to be."

Sheri stepped away from him. She was trying to protect him. "You think that's what I'm doing?"

"Yes, I do. The same as I was doing. The same as Sam was—"

"It's not the same."

"It is. The choices you made stemmed from your past. Sheri, step out on faith. Give it all to God. All of it. The hurt, the resentment. Decide not to let your parents control you for the rest of your life. Sheri, you are so wonderful, if only you knew it. As much as I want you to walk into my arms right now, to marry me, and I want that more than anything, I want even more for you to lean on Christ."

She'd thought she was leaning on Christ. She'd thought taking time to figure out His will in her life was the right step to take…but was it really only her fears continuing to hold her back? She frowned, her thoughts colliding.

Pace suddenly tore his hat off and hung his head for a second. "Wait, what am I saying?" Meeting her gaze with troubled eyes, he reached to touch her hair again but let his hand drop. "God didn't give us a spirit of timidity, but a spirit of power. I believe that. I see it in you. But I got carried away, all I came to say was that I love you and I'll be here if or when you want me. I'm going to go now and leave you alone."

Sheri watched him step back and begin to walk away. He'd quoted the same scripture that Lacy had quoted her earlier. Sheri knew that wasn't a coincidence.

Australia.

The thought brought her up short. She was losing it. There she stood watching Pace, the tall strong man of her dreams walk away. With that little hitch in his stride and that special song in his spurs, and she was thinking about Australia. And how if she ever got the courage to ride a plane the endless hours it would take to get there she'd like to see it….

This was some sort of metaphor for her life. A parallel of different kinds of fear, she realized. She just didn't have the brainpower at the moment to make all the connections.

I did not give you the spirit of fear. Trust me. The words whispered through her soul. *Trust me, Sheri.* Sheri gasped and looked up at the sky. Toward Heaven… God had just spoken to her. To her. Tears sprang to her eyes. It was her gift, her answer to prayers. Trust. Was her trust in herself? Or in God who lived inside her? She had made it all so hard. And it was really so simple.

"Pace." Her voice was weak, but he heard her and spun around, hope shining brightly in his eyes. "For the last few days I've been going over this in my head," she said. "I've been asking the Lord to speak to me. To show me what His plans are for me…all this time everyone, but me, could see it. And I was blind because I wasn't really trusting God." She smiled; she never wanted Pace Gentry walking away from her again.

She met his gaze steady and strong. He stood still,

letting her turn loose a lifetime of fear. And see a lifetime of possibilities. She took a step toward him, holding his gaze as he waited. The way he waited on his horses. The way he gave them room to make a choice. A choice he wanted them to make.

She smiled. Smiled silly, big and wide, and took another step…

Pace opened his arms…and Sheri let go and stepped into her future, trusting God to lead the way.

Epilogue

Pace moved quietly up behind Sheri. She stood on their porch, sipping her evening coffee as she watched the sun setting over the horizon. He slipped his arms around her waist and rested his chin in the crook of her neck, watching with her.

"How is Mrs. Gentry this evening?" He smiled when she leaned her head to rest against his and snuggled deeper into his embrace.

"Mrs. Gentry is awesome now that Mr. Gentry's arms are around her."

"That's good to know, since I don't intend to ever let you go." They'd been married two weeks. Sheri had insisted they get married immediately. Once she'd made up her mind, she went full speed ahead and he'd let her. It worried him at first that she might be acting out of fear, afraid she might get cold feet and back out. But she'd insisted that she felt free and that she didn't need to hang around for weeks or months when she knew what she wanted now. Him. He'd believed her, because he felt the same way and the last two weeks with her as his wife had been the best of his life.

He'd been pleasantly surprised by how much joy she got from helping him with the horses. Her intense interest was a bond he hadn't expected, but he loved it.

"Do you know that I was praying when you snuck up on me?" she whispered against his temple.

He closed his eyes, turned his face to her neck and kissed her there, behind her ear. "About what?"

"About you, us. I was thanking God, one more time. Poor guy, He's probably getting tired of me by now ragging on His ear about how fantastic He is. But I can't help it, Pace. I am so happy. I mean I really am."

She set her cup on the porch railing and turned in his embrace, linking her arms around his neck. "I can't imagine being any happier than I am now. Right this moment."

Overwhelmed, Pace kissed her, his own feelings a mirror image of hers. "I love you, Sheri," he whispered hoarsely, running his fingers through her hair while looking into her sparkling eyes. Then he cleared his throat. "I have something to discuss. Do you think you could take a couple of weeks off from work?"

"In a heartbeat for you. What's up? Another youth retreat?"

"That phone call I had just now was the rancher I worked for back in Idaho."

"Oh yeah. And what did he want?" She nuzzled his neck and kissed his ear.

"He just bought a new ranch and offered me a job."

"A job?" She leaned her head back to look at him.

"A quick job. He wants me to go out to his new ranch and take a look at his horses and work with his cowboys out there. Just for a couple of weeks. A few times a year. It's a good offer. I can still build my own business up here and continue to help Cort with the retreats we're lining up."

"It sounds cool."

He smiled. "Yeah, real cool. I'd just be going out there to make sure things are being done like Mr. Marks wants them done."

"Great. When do we leave? I've wanted to see your Idaho ever since you started telling me about it. We will have so much fun. Can we camp out in a shack in the boonies? Just you, me and the coyotes?"

"Well, how about you, me and the dingoes?"

"What?" Her jaw went slack. "You mean *Australia?*"

"Yeah, I, we, don't have to go." He was alarmed by the look on her face. "I know how you are about flying."

She started laughing and crumpled against him, laughing so hard into the crook of his neck that he had to hang on to her. "What is so funny?" Relieved, he started chuckling, watching her laugh.

She stood up, got her breath and looked at him with dancing eyes. "Oh, Pace. God has the funniest sense of humor. You told me that if I would just trust Him, He would do amazing things."

She started smiling that smile that filled every nook and cranny of his heart, and her eyes sparkled with mischief. The mischief that told him life with Sheri would never be boring.

"He hasn't failed me yet. He gave me you," he said. "So what do you say? Think we can overcome your fear of flying?"

She ran her hand along his jaw, smiling. "With you and God on my side, I say, when do we leave? Australia—ready or not—here I come."

Pace laughed, hugging her to him. Ready or not, would be a fitting way to put things.

* * * * *

A runaway bride's gotta stop running sometime!
Watch Applegate Thornton's granddaughter
meet her match in
OPERATION: MARRIED BY CHRISTMAS
coming from Love Inspired
in October, 2007.

Dear Reader,

I hope you enjoyed *Meeting Her Match* and spending time with me in Mule Hollow!

I loved writing Sheri and Pace's love story. Though I have to say Sheri gave me a hard time. What was I thinking? After all, I wrote the other books. I'd met the sassy gal, so of course I knew she wasn't going to give up her single status easily. However, I didn't know she wasn't exactly who I thought she was. She had a secret. Enter Pace Gentry. What a man! I love heroes who are rough around the edges, but whose hearts are true. And Pace was just the man to help Sheri face her fears and become the woman God intended her to be. And in doing so, he became the man God had set him on the journey to become. They completed each other.

I love that!

And I love that God has blessed me with the opportunity to tell these love stories. If you are enjoying the Mule Hollow books, then come back and celebrate Christmas with us in October 2007. In *Operation: Married by Christmas,* the matchmakers are going to have their hands full when runaway bride Haley Bell Thornton returns home and confronts her past.

As always I love hearing from readers. You can reach me through my Web site debraclopton.com or send a letter to P.O. Box 1125 Madisonville, Texas 77864 or c/o Steeple Hill Books, 233 Broadway, New York, NY 10279.

Until next time keep living, laughing and seeking Christ with all your heart!

Debra Clopton

QUESTIONS FOR DISCUSSION

1. What did you think about this book? Did you relate to any of the characters? In what way?

2. Sheri feels devoted people like Lacy and Adela are more worthy of God's time and attention. Do you feel this way? Why or why not?

3. What do you think about Sheri's attitude? Do you think one's worthiness actually has to do with who is seeking God more?

4. How does God speak to you?

5. I know for me, there are times when God seems silent, but then I realize He's letting me learn something that I need to learn in order to grow as a person and a Christian. Other times I realize I haven't been listening. Has this happened to you? In what way?

6. Obedience isn't always easy. Pace gives up a life he loves to obey God's command that Christians are called out to be salt and light to the world. Have you ever had to give up something you loved in order to be obedient to God? How so?

7. On one hand, Sheri seems to be trying to be someone she isn't. But if she didn't try to be a stronger person, she wouldn't have developed into the woman she is. People frequently say "stop trying to be someone you aren't." What are your thoughts on this?

8. Sheri gives Lacy credit for bringing her out of her shell. But in the end it is trusting herself and realizing that God has plans for her, too, that help her leave the past behind and step toward her future. How have you done something similar in your life?

9. What do you think about the Matchmaking Posse? Do you ever just want to teach someone a lesson? To tell someone to mind their own business? Did it backfire on you?

10. The divorce of Sheri's parents affected her deeply. Sheri learns to let it all go in order to move forward. Are you struggling or have you struggled with something similar in the past? Share your journey with the group.

Love Inspired®

Celebrate Love Inspired's 10th anniversary with top authors and great stories all year long!

FOR HER SON'S LOVE

BY

KATHRYN SPRINGER

A Tiny Blessings Tale

Loving families and needy children continue to come together to fulfill God's greatest plans!

With the legality of her son's adoption in question, Miranda Jones knows she can't trust anyone in Chestnut Grove with her secrets—especially Andrew Noble. He was working his way into her heart, but his investigation into her past could tear her family apart.

Steeple Hill®

Available July wherever you buy books.

Love Inspired®

Celebrate Love Inspired's 10th anniversary with top authors and great stories all year long!

FROM BESTSELLING AUTHOR
JILLIAN HART
COMES A NEW McKASLIN CLAN STORY.

THE McKASLIN CLAN

Lauren McKaslin wanted to reconnect with her family, but mistrustful lawman Caleb Stone stood in her way. Was his attention more than a protective instinct? Now that she believed in family again, perhaps this was also the time to believe in true love.

Look for
A McKASLIN HOMECOMING

Jillian Hart
A McKaslin Homecoming

THE McKASLIN CLAN

Available July wherever you buy books.

REQUEST YOUR FREE BOOKS!

2 FREE INSPIRATIONAL NOVELS
PLUS 2
FREE
MYSTERY GIFTS

LoveInspired®

YES! Please send me 2 FREE Love Inspired® novels and my 2 FREE mystery gifts. After receiving them, if I don't wish to receive any more books, I can return the shipping statement marked "cancel." If I don't cancel, I will receive 4 brand-new novels every month and be billed just $3.99 per book in the U.S., or $4.74 per book in Canada, plus 25¢ shipping and handling per book and applicable taxes, if any*. That's a savings of 20% off the cover price! I understand that accepting the 2 free books and gifts places me under no obligation to buy anything. I can always return a shipment and cancel at any time. Even if I never buy another book from Steeple Hill, the two free books and gifts are mine to keep forever.

113 IDN EF26 313 IDN EF27

Name _____ (PLEASE PRINT) _____

Address _____ Apt. # _____

City _____ State/Prov. _____ Zip/Postal Code _____

Signature (if under 18, a parent or guardian must sign)

Order online at www.LoveInspiredBooks.com

Or mail to Steeple Hill Reader Service™:

IN U.S.A.: P.O. Box 1867, Buffalo, NY 14240-1867
IN CANADA: P.O. Box 609, Fort Erie, Ontario L2A 5X3

Not valid to current Love Inspired subscribers.

Want to try two free books from another series?
Call 1-800-873-8635 or visit www.morefreebooks.com

* Terms and prices subject to change without notice. NY residents add applicable sales tax. Canadian residents will be charged applicable provincial taxes and GST. This offer is limited to one order per household. All orders subject to approval. Credit or debit balances in a customer's account(s) may be offset by any other outstanding balance owed by or to the customer. Please allow 4 to 6 weeks for delivery.

Your Privacy: Steeple Hill is committed to protecting your privacy. Our Privacy Policy is available online at www.eHarlequin.com or upon request from the Reader Service. From time to time we make our lists of customers available to reputable firms who may have a product or service of interest to you. If you would prefer we not share your name and address, please check here. ☐

LIREG07

Love Inspired

TITLES AVAILABLE NEXT MONTH

Don't miss these four stories in July

A McKASLIN HOMECOMING by Jillian Hart
The McKaslin Clan

Lauren McKaslin wanted to reconnect with her family, but mistrustful lawman Caleb Stone stood in her way. Was his attention more than a protective instinct? Now that she believed in family again, perhaps this was also the time to believe in true love.

FOR HER SON'S LOVE by Kathryn Springer
A Tiny Blessings Tale

With the legality of her son's adoption in question, Miranda Jones knows she can't trust anyone in Chestnut Grove with her secrets—especially Andrew Noble. He was working his way into her heart, but his investigation into her past could tear her family apart.

THE PERFECT BLEND by Allie Pleiter
A special Steeple Hill Café novel in Love Inspired

Opening a coffee shop was Maggie Black's dream. She just had to get a loan. Banker William Grey III wanted her to take his business class first, and Maggie agreed. After all, his velvety British accent could make even financial analysis sound interesting.

THE HEART'S FORGIVENESS by Merrillee Whren
Single father Grady Reynolds moved his family to Pinecrest for a fresh start. Instead he found a reminder of the past in Maria Sanchez. She thought helping Grady regain his lost faith would be easy. Except Grady wasn't ready to give or receive forgiveness…or love.

LICNM0607